Love's
Compass
Book Six

Finding Grace

Melanie D. Snitker

John 1:16

Finding Grace
(Love's Compass: Book Six)
© 2018 Melanie D. Snitker

Published by
Dallionz Media, LLC
P.O. Box 6821
Abilene, TX 79608

Cover: Blue Valley Author Services
http://www.bluevalleyauthorservices.com/

Editor: Krista R. Burdine
http://iamgrammaresque.com/

Melanie D. Snitker
melaniedsnitker@gmail.com
www.melaniedsnitker.com

ISBN: 0-9975289-7-4
ISBN-13: 978-0-9975289-7-8

For our daughter, Sydney.
I treasure the moments we spend
having tea parties, reading together,
and talking about our days.
You are beautiful inside and out, and
I'm blessed to be your mommy.
I love you, sweet girl.

Chapter One

L ook, Daddy!"

Tyler Martin instinctively reached for the back of his young daughter's shirt to steady her. Megan stood on the lower rung of the railing, completely oblivious to the eight-foot drop the railing was protecting her from.

Meg pointed to the peacock who was putting on quite the display, his feathers fanned out and glimmering in the sun. "Look! Aren't his feathers pretty?"

"They sure are. Hop down, baby. You don't need to climb on the railing."

Tyler released her shirt as soon as her feet were firmly on the wooden walkway. The raised observation area was a favorite place at the Kitner Zoo. On one side, the small herd of giraffes was visible. On the other, he could see a number of bird habitats along the section below.

The peacock only kept Meg's interest for a few moments before she was on a mission again. She'd talked for days about going to the dock area and feeding the carp.

"Hold on there, Meg. What did we agree on before we got here?"

Meg's lower lip came out. Tyler marveled at how his six-year-old daughter could seem overly mature one moment, and then revert to a pouting mess—albeit a cute one—another. "I really want to see the fish. Can we go now, Daddy? Please?"

"We will see the fish. After we finish looking at the rest of the zoo." She continued to pout, and Tyler frowned. "I suggest you pick up that bottom lip, or we'll go home." Amazing how quickly her scowl disappeared. The stubborn look in her eyes, though, only intensified. Tyler chose to ignore it and led the way toward the other end of the zoo. Meg's little legs moved quickly to keep up, her gaze down on the ground at her feet.

Tyler might have caved and taken her to the fish next if these attitude issues and the lack of listening hadn't been such a common theme lately. He reached for her little hand and held it in his. A moment or two later, he stopped at a bench when he noticed the laces on one of his shoes had come untied. "Hold on, Meg. Let me fix my shoe."

He released her hand, tied his shoe, and turned to speak to Meg.

Except she wasn't there. The empty pavement beside him startled Tyler as surely as a loud noise might have. "Meg?"

He pivoted, taking in the crowd of people around him. He expected to see her waiting only feet away. But there was no sign of her dark hair or the bright pink shirt she was wearing. "Meg!"

A boulder settled in his gut as his heart pounded in his ears. He stepped on a chair and then stood on top of a table to get a better look at the area around him. *God, help me find her. Watch over my baby girl.*

~

Beth Davenport carefully boxed the glass snow globe. She opened a paper bag printed with the Kitner Zoo logo and set the box inside.

"I'll take two of these also, please."

Her customer handed Beth a pair of tiny, plastic flamingos. She scanned them, placed them in an envelope, and added that to the bag. "Is there anything else I can get for you?"

"I think that's it." The older woman smiled brightly and took a wallet out of her purse.

Beth finished ringing up the purchase, relayed the price, and slid the debit card through the reader to finish the transaction. She tucked the receipt inside. "There you go. Thank you for visiting our zoo today. I hope you had a wonderful time."

The other woman tilted her head toward two young children looking at a display with an older gentleman. "We brought the grandkids today, and it was fun. Especially the zoo train. The grandkids enjoyed it, and it gives my old bones a rest." She laughed at her own joke.

Beth smiled and nodded. "I've heard a lot of good things from our visitors. I need to try it myself soon."

She waved goodbye as she watched the group of four leave the gift shop.

Ever since the zoo added the miniature train over

the summer, traffic had increased noticeably. The Kitner Zoo was already a popular attraction, but it was good for business to see so many more visitors coming in.

Monique, one of Beth's coworkers, walked around the counter and locked the main door to the gift shop. It was four in the afternoon, and the zoo wouldn't admit any new guests, but it would be another hour before it closed completely. Customers could still come into the gift shop through the back door that connected it to the zoo.

"Whoo, girl. I'm worn out." Monique rolled her shoulders back dramatically. "It's been non-stop today. I'm ready to go home."

"Me, too." Beth suppressed a yawn. Monique manned the gift shop most days, and Beth often helped her at least a couple days a week. They'd gotten to know each other well over the last two years, and Beth considered Monique a friend.

"When are they going to start training you to lead tours?"

Beth smiled. "A week from Monday." When she'd first started working at the zoo, she'd hoped to help with classes and interact with the children. But what her boss, Chris, needed was someone to help run the gift shop. After diligently doing her job, Beth finally had a chance to expand a little more.

It started out by going along to help load and unload animals when the zookeepers visited the schools. She didn't get to go as often as she'd like to, but her willingness to fill in when needed was noted. Leading tours was just another step toward her goal. The idea that she might be conducting her own tours soon made Beth excited for next week and induced a flock of butterflies fluttering around in her stomach at the same time.

Beth loved her job at the zoo. The variety of tasks appealed to her. She could see the animals every day, interact with people who were there to have fun, and it gave her time in the evenings to write. Eventually, with God's help and the right timing, she hoped to make a living authoring and publishing children's books. Until then, her time at the zoo always fostered more ideas for books than she had time to put on paper.

The back door opened, ushering in the slightly cooler early October breeze. Beth finished stacking some flyers and didn't look up from her task. A minute or two later, she heard a sniff and the sound of someone softly crying. Brows wrinkled, she came around the counter and scanned the inside of the gift shop. No one was in sight.

Another little whimper pulled her to the back wall where stuffed animals lined the shelves. A giant giraffe as tall as Beth stood by a display. Sitting next to it, with her arms wrapped around a plush lion, was a little girl. Tears streaked her face. When she looked up at Beth, her eyes laden with worry and sadness, Beth's heart crumbled.

She knelt in front of the girl she guessed to be five or six. "Hey, sweetie. Where are your parents?"

"I...I can't find my daddy." The girl hiccupped and then wiped her face on the stuffed animal in her arms.

Beth forced herself to not flinch at the mix of moisture on the animal's fur. She sat on the floor next to the girl. "What's your name?"

"Meg." She hiccupped again, but the tears had

slowed.

Monique came around the display, a phone in her hand. "Everything okay?"

Beth tipped her head toward her young charge. "Meg here is lost." She focused on the little girl. "You know what? If you can tell me your daddy's name, I'll bet Monique can find him."

Meg looked hopeful. "Really?"

Monique smiled. "Really." Meg told them his name was Tyler Martin. "Great job. You sit here with Beth, and I'll see what I can do."

"Okay."

Beth reached out and brushed some of the girl's dark hair away from her eyes. "I'll bet your daddy is looking everywhere for you right now. How did you two get separated?"

Meg's gaze fell, and her lower lip stuck out a little. "I got mad and left when he wasn't watching. Then I couldn't find him again."

A memory from when Beth was a girl not much younger than Meg resurfaced. "I did something like that when I was your age. I have an older brother and three older sisters, and I got jealous when it seemed like they were helping my mom shop more than I could. When no one was looking, I ran away from the basket and hid down one of the aisles. I thought it would make my mommy feel bad, and she'd give me more to do." She gave an exaggerated frown. "But guess what?" She barely heard the page go out across the zoo announcing the missing girl.

Meg cuddled the lion to her. "What?"

"It did make her feel bad, but I think I felt even worse." She could still remember the way Mom cried when they finally found each other again. Beth didn't think she'd ever forget the look on her face. "I was so scared, I never did that again."

The girl took in a shaky breath. "I'm never going to run away again, either."

"That's good, I'm glad to hear it." She stood and had reached for Meg's hand to help her up when the door to the gift shop whooshed open.

A man looked around the room, his movements frantic. "I heard the page. I'm Tyler Martin. Meg's here? You have her?"

"Daddy!"

Meg dropped the stuffed lion. She made her way through the obstacle course of displays and jumped into the man's arms.

Beth followed, a smile tugging her lips upward as she watched the reunion.

Tyler set his daughter down, knelt to her level, and gave her a stern look. "Don't you ever do that again, young lady. I don't care how mad you get, you don't run off like that. Am I understood?"

Meg's chin drifted down, and she bobbed her head slowly.

"I can't hear you."

"Yes, sir."

Beth's heart went out to Tyler. She could only imagine how much of a nightmare it must've been for him to discover his child missing.

Tyler cupped his daughter's face in his hands. "If you promise to not let go of my hand, we can finish looking at the zoo. What do you think?"

Meg nodded again and held on tight.

He stood, lifting his daughter into his arms. Only then did his gaze stray from her face. He noticed Beth for the first time, and his eyebrows rose as he strode forward. "I'm sorry about that. I blinked, and she was gone."

Beth took in the short beard and mustache. They fit him and made him look sophisticated. She studied his eyes, amazed at how dark brown they were. She forced herself to stop staring at them. "Kids are fast. Trust me, it happens more than you'd think here. I'm glad you two were reunited this quickly." It was clear Meg resembled her father. Both had hair that was nearly black, the same nose, and a clear love for each other. But where his eyes were dark, Meg's were green. Beth reached out to pat Meg on the back. "Your daughter was smart to run in here instead of wandering around outside or going to the parking lot."

"Trust me, I won't be letting this girl out of my sight from now on." He ran his large left hand over Meg's hair. His nails were neatly trimmed and there was ink or something similar in the nailbeds. Beth noticed he didn't wear a wedding ring.

Not that it mattered. She stopped staring at his hand and turned her attention to his face. He gave her a small smile then, and the lighter expression lit up his eyes.

"I'm more than relieved you found Meg. I can't thank you enough."

His gaze tangled with hers for several moments before Beth cleared her throat. The heat of embarrassment climbed her neck. What was wrong with her? "Not a problem."

Tyler nodded to Monique, said thank you, and looked at Beth again. "I guess we'll be heading home. Here's to a less eventful evening for us all."

Beth chuckled. She waved at their backs as they walked through the door and disappeared. She didn't hear Monique approach until her coworker spoke from nearby. "I didn't think they made dads that hot."

The comment brought out a short laugh from Beth. She gave her friend a good-natured roll of her eyes. "Come on, we've got fifteen minutes left. Let's get this place closed up. I, for one, am ready to call it a day."

She walked back to the front and craned her neck to look out the windows. There was no sign of Tyler and Meg.

Half an hour later, the coworkers walked together to the parking lot. Monique waved. "See you tomorrow?"

"I'll be here." Beth unlocked her Corolla and got inside. Even though the air was cool, the Texas sun had still managed to heat up the inside of her car. She turned the key and gritted her teeth when it took a moment or two longer than usual for the engine to turn over. She flipped the air conditioner on and pulled out of her parking spot.

Her mind went back to earlier events. She couldn't stop thinking about the way Tyler protectively held his daughter. She may not have seen a wedding ring on his finger, but there was no way a guy like him wasn't attached to someone.

Loneliness crept in. Like always, it happened when Beth least expected it. She frowned. Spending evenings alone was a small price to pay if it meant avoiding a repeat of her last relationship. Breaking up with Carl had been one of the best things she'd ever done. It was too bad the emotional scars from their time together didn't disappear as quickly as he had.

~

Tyler kissed Meg on the forehead. "I love you, baby. Get some sleep."

"Good night, Daddy." She put an arm around her stuffed giraffe and hugged it close. Her eyes drifted closed, her dark lashes creating feathery crescents against her skin.

His heart squeezed. She was his whole world. If something had happened to her today...

He stood and shoved the disconcerting thoughts aside. *Thank you, Father, for watching over her when I couldn't.* He eased her door closed and headed to the living room. His dad, Bill, was lounging in the recliner, his glasses halfway down the bridge of his nose as he read the newspaper. He looked up over the rims. "She asleep?"

"Yep." Tyler flopped onto the couch and put his feet up on the coffee table. "I don't know what she was thinking running off like that." His emotions had ping-ponged between anger and relief all evening.

"She wasn't, only reacting. You were all over the place at six, and I hear girls are even more emotional."

"Wonderful." He groaned and let his head hit the back of the couch. "I've got my work cut out for me, don't I?"

Dad chuckled. "You sure do."

Tyler shot his dad a stern look. Truthfully, Dad had been more help than any son could possibly hope for. But there were times like these when Tyler wished his mom was still here. Surely, she would have some sage advice about how he was supposed to deal with these new issues of Meg's. She was his little buddy, and that'd always been enough before. Lately, though, she'd been having attitude problems.

Tyler could deal with the occasional lying or emotional outbursts. What he hadn't handled well were her questions about why her mother, Reece, wasn't around. He'd tried to explain that families are set up differently and not every child has both a mom and dad in the home. Every time Meg brought up the subject, her questions got more and more difficult to answer.

Most days he thought he had this whole single parenting thing figured out. And then Meg threw him a curveball like she did today.

Tyler groaned. "Should I ground her?"

Dad folded the newspaper, slapped it on his knee, and laughed out loud. "From what? Going to first grade? Playing on the tree swing? I think being lost and scared probably made enough of an impression for a six-year-old." He pushed his glasses up higher on his nose. "Things will be fine, son. She's home and safe."

"Yeah." The woman at the gift shop was right. Praise God Meg had decided to go in there instead of wandering to the parking lot or somewhere else on the zoo grounds. He'd been so shaken by losing Meg that he hadn't even bothered to ask the woman what her name was.

He could still picture her blonde hair and those impossibly blue eyes. Praise God she'd been kind enough to check on his daughter and make sure she was okay. "Do you think I should thank her?"

"Who's that?" Dad had moved on to reading the sports section, his brow furrowed in concentration.

"The lady who found Meg. Do you think I should go back and thank her?"

"Didn't you do that when you picked Meg up?" Dad looked up from what he was reading and gave Tyler a questioning look. "You got the hots for her or something?"

Tyler rolled his eyes. It'd been way too long of a day for this. The humor in Dad's expression wasn't helping. "What are you, Dad? Fifteen?"

"At heart. I think that counts for something."

Okay, he had to give him that. "No, I was just so worried when I found Meg that I didn't ask her what her name was. I'm pretty sure I said thank you, but I can't even guarantee that. She played a hand in saving your granddaughter. I think I should go by and thank her."

"Then do that. Go express your gratitude tomorrow, and I'll handle the shop for a while. No big deal."

"You sure?"

"Yep." He went back to his newspaper.

Tyler thought about it a moment and then nodded to himself. He'd go back tomorrow, find the woman who watched out for Meg, and thank her for being such a big help. Maybe even take her to lunch.

Where had that thought come from? She might think he was asking her out on a date, and that wasn't going to happen. He hadn't dated since Reece and had no intention of starting now. Things were complicated enough being a single dad without trying to throw a relationship into the mix. He couldn't fathom watching another woman walk away from him. From Meg.

He'd go, tell her thank you, and that would be it.

Tyler refused to acknowledge the way the thought of seeing her again caused his heart to do a little jig.

Chapter Two

Tyler wiped his greasy hands on a rag and stepped away from the car he'd been working on. They'd spent several days rebuilding the engine, a project that'd taken longer than anticipated. He looked across the garage to his dad who was installing new brakes on a Jeep Wrangler. "How's it going over there?"

"Great." Dad peeked at the watch on his left wrist. "It's nearly lunchtime. You should head over to the zoo if you're going to."

"Yeah. I guess I will. Call me if something comes up. Want me to pick up sandwiches on my way back?"

"Grab me a roast beef."

Tyler waved and headed to the sink at the back of the garage. He washed his hands as best he could, though no amount of scrubbing ever completely eliminated the grease around the edges or beneath his fingernails. He grabbed one of the clean T-shirts he kept stored in the office, changed, and headed out to his 4Runner.

He probably should've called the zoo to see if she was working today. But he wasn't entirely sure how to accomplish that when he didn't even know her name. Instead, he'd drive the fifteen minutes over there and hope he could find her.

The parking lot was over half full, which seemed busy for mid-Monday. Tyler parked his vehicle, raked his fingers through his hair, and strode to the gift shop.

A voice spoke up from the other side of the counter. "Welcome to Kitner Zoo. Can I help you find anything?" Her name tag had "Monique" printed on it.

Tyler's gaze swung to Monique who watched him expectantly and couldn't help but be disappointed she wasn't who he was looking for. "Hi. Yeah, I was here yesterday. My little girl was lost, and I was hoping to thank the woman who found her."

Monique smiled. "Of course! I remember you. That was Beth. She's actually on an early lunch right now."

I knew I should've called. Had Beth worn a name tag yesterday? If so, he hadn't noticed. "All right. Well, it was a long shot to catch her, anyway." He jerked a thumb toward the door he'd passed through. "I'll try another time."

"You know, she takes her lunch here at the zoo. I'm sure she wouldn't mind if you want to go on through and find her. She almost always eats at a shaded table near the jaguars." She gave him a wink.

"You're sure? Do I need to pay for a ticket?"

"Nah. Go on."

Tyler grinned. "I appreciate it. I won't be here long, I need to get back to work soon."

"Take your time."

He pushed the door open and stepped into the

sunlight. He'd taken Meg to the zoo at least a half-dozen times and knew which tables Monique referred to. The zoo itself wasn't overly large, and it didn't take long to reach the jaguars. He put a hand over his eyes to block the sun and scanned the area.

A woman sat with her back to him, her blonde hair braided into a rope that hung below the top of her chair. She leaned over the table in front of her. Even though he couldn't see her face, Tyler knew it was Beth. As he got close enough to study her profile, it was clear she was concentrating on the small laptop she furiously typed on.

Tyler walked up to the table and cleared his throat.

Beth lifted her chin and squinted at him. He shifted to block the sliver of sun that shone around the umbrella above them. When she got a good look at him, her eyes widened in surprise. He'd remembered them being blue, but they were even brighter than the picture in his mind. Without looking down, she used her left hand to close the laptop.

"Hi. Tyler Martin, right?"

She remembered his name. That fact probably mattered way more than it should. "Yes." He held a hand out. "And you're Beth?"

"Beth Davenport." She shook his hand briefly before placing both of hers in her lap.

"Yesterday was crazy, and I admit I was more than a little rattled. I'm afraid I didn't properly thank you for what you did for my daughter." He paused. "I don't want to think about what might have happened if you hadn't found her."

She shook her head as a blush painted her cheeks a pretty shade of pink. "I didn't do much. Just sat with her while Monique had you paged. It wasn't a big deal."

"You're wrong about that. Meg said you made her feel better. That means a lot to me. To us." He glanced at her hands and noted there was no wedding ring. How was a woman as beautiful and kind as her not spoken for?

His own thoughts surprised him. Why did it matter whether she was married or not?

They both stared at each other for several breaths, and Tyler searched for something to say. He ought to thank her again and take his leave. He noticed the sandwich and chips on the table and the silver laptop with a variety of stickers decorating the top of it. The combination of super heroes and butterflies nearly had him smiling. She was clearly trying to relax during her lunch. With his hands buried deep in his pockets, Tyler opened his mouth to say good bye. "Meg and I go to get ice cream every Monday after school. Would you care to join us? We'd like to buy you a dish to thank you for your help." Where had that come from?

The shock on her face probably mirrored his own. "Oh, I...I probably shouldn't. I have to work until five. I wouldn't want you to have to wait on me."

"Of course." He shouldn't have even invited her. It made sense she'd be working. Tyler took his wallet out of his pocket and withdrew a business card. "My dad and I own Martin Mechanics. If you ever have car trouble, don't hesitate to call me. Us." Wow, he kept digging the hole deeper.

"Thank you." She reached for it, her fingers brushing his.

The last thing he expected was the trail of electricity that extended from her touch straight to his heart. She jerked the card toward her, and he wondered if she'd felt it, too.

"Sure. I'll let you get back to your lunch. Maybe Meg and I'll see you next time we come to the zoo."

A small smile lifted the corners of her mouth, bringing a sparkle to her eyes. "Sounds good. Have a great day, Tyler."

"You, too, Beth." He waved at her, and with some effort, turned and walked away.

He'd handed her a business card that would hopefully result in some word-of-mouth business. That was the plan, right? He tried to do the same thing every time he met someone new. But this was different.

This time, it felt like he'd given his phone number to a pretty girl instead.

~

Beth propped her phone between her shoulder and her ear. "Yeah, Mom. Of course." She pulled the gray towel off her head, and her wet hair tumbled down. The cold ends quickly soaked through her cotton shirt. "What do you want me to bring?"

"How about some balloons? Oh! And a veggie plate."

"Dad never eats raw veggies. Do you really think he will during his birthday party?" Beth teased.

"Maybe not. But at sixty, he needs more vegetables in his diet."

That might be, but Beth doubted Dad would start eating them now. Still, ever since he had a stroke two and a half years ago, they'd all been watchful of his eating and exercising habits. The fact was, every birthday was something to celebrate. "I'll get the vegetables, Mom." Along with some ranch dip and maybe French onion to make them palatable.

"Wonderful. Thanks, Bethie. I've got your brother and sisters bringing something too. It should be fun! Dad knows I'm throwing him a birthday party, but he doesn't know you're all going to be there."

"He's going to love it, Mom."

"I think so too. Okay, I have to let you go. I need to call Gwen and make sure they'll be able to make the drive. She thought they would, but since Cade is so little, you just never know."

Beth thought about her baby nephew and smiled. She couldn't wait to cuddle him and the rest of her nieces and nephews in less than two weeks. "I'll talk to you soon. Love you."

"Love you too. Bye."

Beth hung up and tossed her phone on the bed. She stared at her reflection in the mirror. She'd spent the last week training to give tours at the zoo. Today, they were letting her guide a group on her own. She couldn't decide if she were more excited or nervous. Not only that, but her boss said she may be able to go on a school visit Wednesday. It was shaping up to be a great week.

Her gaze went to the laptop whirring quietly on her desk. She'd spent years jotting down ideas or writing half of a story only to move on to another one. It was weird to think about how many hours of her life were solely represented by files on a hard drive. In the past, every time she tried to finish a book and move to the next phase, something would stop her. She'd doubt it was good enough, or another story would battle for her attention. One thing after the other kept pushing her timeline back.

Her ex's voice echoed in her head as she remembered how he'd ridiculed her dream of becoming an author. She'd finally gained enough courage to print out her story and had given it to Carl to read. After waiting, pacing the floor in nervous anticipation, he'd finally lowered the papers and frowned.

"This is a waste of time. You can't make money, you're not nearly good enough. You should focus on your day job and leave writing to the real authors."

His words planted seeds of doubt, and they still stung. They'd made her wonder how she could possibly write and publish something kids would want to read. She'd started to think he might be right. After all, she hadn't shared her stories with anyone else until then. If the first person to read them hated them that much...

His less-than-supportive comments were only the beginning, though. If she'd known how much worse things would get, she wouldn't have let those words damage her confidence like they had.

Beth shut down her train of thought, unwilling to relive that last month she and Carl were together.

If nothing else, their relationship had served one purpose: It had convinced Beth she needed to quit wasting time. She wanted to write picture books for children and publish them. There was no time like the present.

A month after the break-up, she did a lot of research, eventually deciding to publish her books independently. From there, she chose an illustrator she liked and sent him the finished story she'd shown Carl along with some ideas of the images she'd like on each page.

Her illustrator loved the whole idea. Since then, she'd approved a couple of sample images. He promised to get the rest back to her by the end of October. Every time she checked her e-mail, she held her breath with nervous anticipation.

She'd been working on the next book when Tyler found her at the zoo the previous week. He was the last person she'd expected to see. She smiled as she thought about their brief visit. There was something about those dark eyes of his that drew her in. Maybe he'd bring Meg back to the zoo again soon.

The zoo. She'd better quit procrastinating and get to work. Everyone she talked to assured her the tours got easier each time. She just needed to survive the first solo run and she'd be fine. It was a good thing her zoo uniform T-shirt was black with the way she was sweating right now.

Beth arrived at the zoo, secured her things in the gift shop area, and said hello to Monique. Her coworker gave her a mock frown. "I still can't believe you're going to leave me to handle this place on my own most of this week. You ready for show time?"

"As ready as I'll ever be. I hope I don't get tongue tied or forget all the facts I've spent two weeks memorizing."

"You'll be fine. Put on that famous smile, turn on the Beth charms, and you'll have them eating out of the palm of your hand. It worked on that little girl's dad, didn't it?" She winked and gave Beth a knowing look.

"What happy pill did you take this morning? Are you sharing?"

Monique only laughed and turned to help a customer at the ticket window.

Beth shook her head. Monique had no idea what she was talking about. Sure, Tyler was handsome. Cute, even. But she'd likely never see him again. The fact that she'd come to work every day the last week hoping to see him meant absolutely nothing. And that quickening of her heart rate? Purely a result of her frayed nerves and their response to the upcoming tour.

The group waiting for her had at least twenty-five people in it. As she approached, she said a silent prayer to calm her nerves. They seemed happy to see her, though, which gave her a boost of confidence. When she first began to lead them through the zoo, she spoke way too quickly and kept having to suck in breaths of air. But by the time it ended thirty minutes later, she was speaking more slowly and wasn't feeling quite as nervous. No one appeared bored or annoyed, and Beth hadn't thrown up on anyone's shoes. As far as she was concerned, she deserved a check mark in the win column.

She led the group back to the gift shop, thanked them all for coming, and released a lungful of air. *You did it, girl. See, you've got this. Tours? No problem.*

Beth seriously considered celebrating with something chocolate. A candy bar. Maybe ice cream.

The second the word ice cream popped into her head, an image of Tyler joined it, and she groaned. Last Monday, he said he took his daughter to get the treat every week. Were they going again today after school? More than once, Beth wished she could've taken him up on the kind offer to join them. She couldn't very well go from ice cream shop to ice cream shop looking for them now, especially when the father and daughter were likely going to be finished and home again before she even got off work.

She had no business thinking about Tyler, anyway. He might have been a whimsical distraction, but it was time to push him from her daydreams and focus on something more realistic. Like coming up with ways to deflect her family's inquisitions about her love life at Dad's birthday party.

Chapter Three

Beth helped Tate, one of the zookeepers, double check that all four cages were secure. Hermione, the large macaw rocking back and forth in her traveling enclosure, looked excited. Of all the different animals that rotated in and out for events, Hermione seemed to enjoy the experience the most.

Tate nodded toward the door. "I think we're good to go."

Beth stepped outside the classroom and held up a hand until everyone's attention was on her. "All right, kids. Are you ready to learn about some amazing animals today?"

"Yeah!" The enthusiastic voices echoed off the walls.

"Awesome! Now, I need your help. When you come inside, be as quiet as you can so that you don't scare the animals. Do we have a deal?" The kids nodded silently. "Perfect." She propped the door open then and stood back as teachers led their students inside. Once it seemed like everyone was settled, she closed it again. She was on her way back to the front when she heard what sounded like her name in a whisper. Beth stopped and scanned the room.

"Pssst! Beth!"

A little waving hand drew Beth's attention to young Meg sitting near the front of the room. The girl's face lit up with a smile when Beth waved back.

She'd thought about Tyler a lot, but hadn't even considered the possibility she'd see his daughter on this outing. She scanned the room to ensure he wasn't one of the adults in attendance, then fought the wave of disappointment when she didn't see him.

The presentation went well. Beth's main job was to help Tate get the animals in and out of the cages. She also made sure the kids didn't get too close and reminded them to keep the noise down.

The room filled with "oohs" and "aahs" when Tate brought out the bearded dragon named Toothless. They laughed at Hermione the macaw and her antics. It took a little extra coaxing to get the bird back in her cage when her time was up, much to the delight of the children.

Zip the black footed ferret was next, his bright eyes and twitching nose always a crowd-pleaser. When Tate finished telling the children about the ferret and his habitat, he handed him over to Beth. She held the rambunctious animal in the crook of her arm.

Finally, Tate waited until everyone had quieted down. "We only have one more animal to show you. Now, Tilly may be large, but she can be shy. We have to use our inside voices. Do you all think you can do that?"

Lots of nods and hushed affirmations filled the room. Tate reached into the last cage and carefully lifted the albino Burmese python eliciting excited gasps from the children.

Tate told them facts about Tilly while the snake curled around his arm. "Believe it or not, Tilly here is still young. That's right, when she's full grown, she may be twice as long as I am tall."

Zip had settled into the warmth of Beth's shirt and looked ready to doze. The little guy was nocturnal and probably more than ready to get back to bed.

"Now," Tate continued, "if you'll listen to your teachers and make two lines, you can come up and pet either Tilly here or Zip." It was no surprise that there were more girls in the line for Zip, and more boys in the line for Tilly.

Beth instructed each child on how to pet Zip as they came to the front of the line. Five minutes in, Meg appeared, all smiles. "I was so excited to see you, Beth! And Zip is soooo cute! I'm going to tell Daddy that we have to get a pet ferret." She put a single finger out and ran it along Zip's back. "His fur is so soft."

"Isn't he, though?" Beth tilted her head toward Tilly. "You didn't want to see the snake?"

Meg wrinkled her nose in the cutest way. "No. I'm not a snake fan."

Beth lowered her voice. "Me, either. You know what? If you want to ask your teacher for permission and then wait right over there by the blackboard, you can help me put Zip back in his cage when we're done."

Meg's eyes widened right along with her smile. "Okay!" She skipped off to one of the adults standing nearby.

The rest of the kids finished petting the animals and were led, single file, from the room. A teacher stayed behind to wait for Meg and the boy Tate chose to help him get Tilly settled into her cage.

Beth beckoned to Meg. "Do you remember how Tate said ferrets are nocturnal?" Meg nodded. "That means that poor Zip here is tired and probably ready to go to bed." The ferret seemed content to remain in Beth's arms.

"I wish I could hold him."

"I'd let you if I could. But what I need you to do is open the cage. I'll put him in, and then you close it again before he can sneak out. Do you think you can do that?" Meg gave another enthusiastic nod.

Zip was more than happy to climb right in and curl up in the hammock hanging across the bottom of the cage. Meg closed the door, Beth made sure it was secure, and then covered the cage with a dark cloth.

"That was awesome! Thanks for letting me help you, Beth."

"You're welcome, Meg. Now you'd better run, it looks like your teacher is waiting."

She threw her arms around Beth in a big hug. "I hope I get to see you again soon."

"I hope so." And Beth meant it. There was something about the sweet girl that made Beth's day brighter. "Work hard today."

"I will. Bye!"

"Bye." Beth waved and watched as the teacher escorted both students from the room.

~

For whatever reason, Thursday tended to pass much slower at the zoo. As a result, Beth had that day and Sunday off every week. Some people said they were sorry when they heard she worked on Saturdays, but Beth didn't mind. She liked having Thursdays off instead. It meant she could go shopping when the stores weren't as busy, and it was easier to make appointments.

It also meant she had the opportunity to have lunch with her sister, Avalon, and Beth's young niece, Lorelei. Ever since Avalon and her husband, Duke, moved back to Kitner almost two years ago, Beth had made a point of visiting her sister for lunch at least once a month. Out of her four siblings, Avalon was the closest to Beth in age, and they'd always gotten along well. It was a huge bonus to get Lorelei all to herself during their lunch dates instead of having to share her with their large extended family.

She swung by Daisy Belle's Diner to pick up some soup, salad, and rolls then headed for Duke and Avalon's house. She reached the door, her hands full of food bags, when Avalon opened it.

"Hey, Beth. Come on in. You're a life saver. It's been one of those days, and I've been looking forward to this all week." Avalon shifted giving Beth enough room to slip inside.

"Me, too." Beth set the bags down on the kitchen table. "My car's been making a funny sound. I need to take it in and get it checked out." She kept forgetting about it except for when she was actually driving the car. An excited baby squeal came from the other room and brought a grin to Beth's face. "Where's my niece hiding?"

"I'm getting her. I had to vacuum and this little one can't stay out of trouble for more than thirty seconds." Her voice faded before Avalon appeared again with Lorelei in her arms. The moment the sixteen-month-old cutie saw Beth, she threw her arms wide and nearly squirmed away from Avalon.

Beth laughed. "Come to your favorite aunt, Rory." She hugged the little one to her chest and patted her on the back.

"You know you're still the only one who calls her that."

"It's my pet name for her." Beth shrugged. "Besides, you know one of my favorite shows is 'Gilmore Girls', what did you expect?" She tickled Lorelei's tummy and was rewarded with giggles. "Are you hungry? I got that bread you like." She set Lorelei down on the floor and watched as the little girl ran to her highchair and proceeded to climb up and into it like a champ.

Avalon gestured to her daughter and then buckled her in. "You see why I can't turn my back on the girl?"

"No kidding."

They got settled with some lunch. Avalon took a bite of her salad and released a happy sigh. "Gotta love Daisy's homemade ranch dressing and her soup. You know, her diner was one of the things I missed the most while living in Arizona. Outside of family, of course."

"Of course."

Avalon had gone to school in Arizona, met and married Duke, and then the couple moved back to Kitner when Avalon was about halfway through her pregnancy with Lorelei. Beth couldn't have been happier to have them local again.

They ate in comfortable silence for a few moments before Avalon spoke again. "So, what's new in your life? I haven't seen you much since the last time we had lunch."

It didn't seem like Beth ever had much in the way of news to report. Sad, right? She shrugged. "Work. They have me leading tours now."

Avalon's grinned. "That's great! Any idea whether they'll be letting you help with the zoo classes?"

"Nothing yet. I'm going to lead as many tours as I can and hope they'll consider letting me serve as an aid during the summer camps." Beth used a finger to swipe a drip of dressing from her plate and licked it off.

"Any news from the illustrator?"

Beth shrugged. "No. I should hear back soon, though." She smiled at Lorelei. Maybe one day Beth would read the picture book to her.

"How about guys? I don't suppose that's why we haven't heard as much from you, is it?"

Beth held her breath for several heartbeats. She hated it when her family asked her about men. There'd been a lot of reasons why she didn't like to discuss the topic, and Carl was right there at the top. Her family knew about him and how horrible the relationship had been. It didn't matter that Beth was sure she'd rather be single for the rest of her life than risk a repeat performance; her family insisted she needed to put her fears aside and start dating again. They meant well, but she wished they'd let the whole subject drop.

"Sorry to disappoint you. The closest I've come to a date is eating lunch with the jaguars."

Avalon didn't look happy about that. "It's been what? Six months since Carl? You can't let a creep like him dictate the rest of your life. It's time you started dating again. You're not getting any younger, you know."

"Gee, thanks for that." Beth took another bite of

her loaded baked potato soup. "You know I don't like talking about Carl. I'm good with my life right now, Avalon." *Mostly.* "Don't push things."

Her sister held up both hands in surrender. "Okay. Just be prepared for the third degree at Dad's birthday. You know Marian. She's got to make sure everyone is experiencing happy-ever-after like she and Jason are."

"I know." Beth hoped having all the family together would take the spotlight off her. If only she could be that lucky.

And luck rarely was on her side. She'd have to deal with dodging the boyfriend questions until everyone found some other family news to grab on to.

When she was around her family and saw all her siblings happily married, most of them with children of their own, she had to fight against the sadness. She'd love to have what they did, if only her next relationship was guaranteed to work out. But heaven knew there were no guarantees where love was concerned.

~

"You've got to be kidding." Beth let her forehead rest against the steering wheel of her car. She'd been trying to get the engine to turn over for the last fifteen minutes to no avail. This is what she got for putting off taking her car to a mechanic.

Monique was already gone, and it was Friday evening. That meant her brother, Lance, was home with his wife, Lexi. Duke, Avalon, and Lorelei were probably sitting down to dinner. And Beth didn't want to interrupt Mom and Dad to ask them for help.

Besides, what were they going to do if the car

wouldn't run? She'd still have to have the vehicle towed anyway. She'd do that first, then she could call for a ride home.

She stared at her purse for several moments before finally reaching for it and withdrawing her wallet.

Yes, she'd kept the business card Tyler Martin had given her. Why shouldn't she? Obviously having the phone number for a local mechanic was going to come in handy. She'd nearly thrown it away at least a dozen times, and it's a good thing she hadn't. Beth almost felt validated in her weird need to keep the card tucked into one of the back slots of her wallet.

She dialed the number and waited through two rings before someone answered.

"Martin Mechanics, this is Bill, how can we help you?"

This man sounded older. Didn't Tyler say he ran it with his dad?

Beth filled him in on her situation. "The car needs to be towed. If you guys can handle the repairs there, that would be awesome."

"We have a tow truck and would be happy to repair your car." There was some shuffling of papers in the background. "Let me get all of your contact information, and someone will be there with the tow truck in the next thirty minutes."

Beth relaxed against her seat. She hadn't realized until then how tense she'd been. "Great. Thank you."

She gave him all her information and then waited for the tow truck. Once it got there, she could call Avalon or Lance and have someone give her a ride home.

Bill was true to his word. Less than twenty

minutes had gone by before a tow truck pulled into the zoo parking lot, the headlights bright in the dimming daylight. She'd convinced herself to expect Bill or someone else from the shop she didn't know. She stepped out of the car, slipped her hands into her pockets, and leaned against the door.

The tow truck stopped in front of her vehicle. Beth couldn't quite make out who was sitting in the driver's seat until that door opened and the man stepped to the ground. She sucked in a breath as Tyler's familiar face appeared, complete with that smile she hadn't been able to get out of her head since she first met him.

Come on, Beth, keep it cool. He's here to tow your car, no need to come off looking like an idiot.

~

Tyler couldn't count the number of times he'd thought about Beth since he'd last spoken with her. It'd been a week and a half, but her face and soft voice entered his head when he least expected it.

He'd resigned himself to never seeing her again. The last thing he'd expected was for Meg to hop into his 4Runner on Wednesday raving about how Beth had come with the man from the zoo, and she even let Meg help with the ferret. Tyler wasn't real clear about what happened, but it was obvious it'd made a huge impression on his daughter.

He'd been trying to decide whether he should take Meg back to the zoo again soon or not. They normally only visited a couple of times a year. To go twice in one month would put Dad on the alert, not that he wasn't already.

That's when Dad had broken through Tyler's reverie and handed him some paperwork.

"There's a woman at the zoo who is stranded and needs a tow. A Beth Davenport, I believe," Dad had said, one bushy eyebrow raised and a twinkle in his eye. He insisted he'd get Meg ready for bed if Tyler would take care of the call.

Now Tyler was on his way to the zoo. If Beth called the shop, did that mean she'd remembered the name of their place? Or had she hung onto the business card he gave her? Part of him hoped it was the latter, and then he immediately wanted to kick some sense into himself.

He drove into the zoo's parking lot. It was nearly dark, and Tyler didn't like the idea of Beth out there alone. Thankfully, it looked like she'd stayed in the car until he arrived. By the time he got out of the tow truck, she was standing outside.

Tyler waved with a smile. "Hey! I hear you're having some trouble."

"I am, thank you for coming." Beth motioned to her car. "It won't start."

"Has anyone tried to jump the battery?"

She shook her head, her blonde hair catching some of what little ambient light was left in the day. "No."

"Let's give that a try first. If we're lucky, it'll start right up, and you won't have to have it towed."

Beth gave him a nod, the stress on her face easing a little at the suggestion.

He got the cables out of the back seat but charging the battery made no difference. "Well, it was worth a try. Towing it is. You can sit in the truck while I load your car if you'd like, and I'll give you a ride back to the office."

"That's great."

Tyler held the passenger door open for her, waited for her to get settled, and closed it again.

He had the car loaded and ready to go as quickly as possible. When he got into the cab of the truck himself, there was no missing the combination of a scent that reminded him of tropical fruit, yet had a completely unique undertone. Something wonderfully feminine that all but erased the usual traces of motor oil. He put the truck in gear and steered them through the empty parking lot.

"I should be able to look at your car tomorrow. As soon as I know what's going on with it, I'll give you a call. Hopefully it'll be something minor. We won't make any repairs until we've spoken with you first and given you an estimate."

"I appreciate it." Beth pulled a phone out of her purse. "Let me call my brother and have him come pick me up at your shop." After withdrawing her wallet, she took the Martin Mechanics business card out, probably for the address.

Well, the business card answered his earlier question. And her brother? Tyler tried not to assume it meant she wasn't seeing someone. He suppressed a smile. "I'm going to secure your car in the yard and head home. I'd be happy to drop you off at your place on the way. Where do you live?"

Beth looked less than certain. "Off Oak Street."

"I'm serious—that's on my way home." Would he normally offer a customer a ride to their house after towing their vehicle? Absolutely. Did it usually matter this much whether the customer accepted the offer? Not really.

She hesitated. "Are you sure? I wouldn't want to delay you getting home to Meg."

"I'm sure. She's with her grandfather and probably thrilled to have bedtime pushed back a little." He chuckled.

"All right. I appreciate it."

Her acceptance of his offer left him feeling happier than it should have. They got to the shop, Tyler secured her car in the fenced-in lot, had Beth fill out her contact information, and then led her to his 4Runner. He glanced at her and began their trek to her place. "You know, Meg can't stop talking about your visit to the school. I'm not sure if she was more impressed with the ferret or you."

Beth chuckled. "I always enjoy the opportunity to go with Tate to schools. It was sweet of Meg to go out of her way to say hi. Inviting her to help me put Zip back in his cage was the least I could do."

"Well, first you rescue her at the zoo. Then you swoop in and make her day. I think you may be her super hero." Meg didn't get a lot of female attention and was desperately in need of it. It meant a lot to Tyler that Beth was taking the time to include Meg and make her feel special.

The ride to Beth's place was going way too fast; they'd be there in another minute or two. "I saw an ad about the trick-or-treating event at the zoo. I've never taken Meg to it before, but we were hoping to do something different this year. What do you think about it? Does it get crowded?"

"It does. But the event runs from ten in the morning until six that evening. If you go before one, it won't be nearly as busy. I like this event for trick-or-treating because it takes place during the daylight hours. Makes it easier to keep track of the little monsters."

Tyler could barely see the amusement in her eyes and laughed. "Yeah, daylight is definitely the way to go with Meg." He paused. "Will you be working that day?"

"I will." She looked at him and then back at the lights going by her window. "I'll be handing out candy at a station near the giraffes until about two."

"Good to know." That sounded lame. "It's nice you don't have to work all day. I imagine that would be a long one."

"I normally would. But my family's celebrating my dad's sixtieth birthday that evening. I scheduled to have the afternoon and evening off months ago."

They reached her apartment complex. He pulled into the parking lot and followed her directions to her building. "Here we are."

"Thanks again for the ride. And for picking up my car."

"It's not a problem. I can walk you to your door if you'd like."

She smiled again. "Nah, I'm good."

"In that case, you have a good night, Beth."

"You, too, Tyler." She gave him a little wave, got out of the truck, and walked away.

Tyler exhaled and headed home.

He'd have to think about it, but something told him he'd be taking Meg to the zoo for Halloween this year.

Chapter Four

What do you think, Daddy?" Meg ran into the living room dressed in her Wonder Woman costume. She stopped, flexed her arms, and pasted a serious look on her face. "I wish we could go trick-or-treating *today*. I think I've been waiting for years and years."

Tyler fought back a chuckle. "Honey, you've had that costume five days. And you'll be gathering more candy than you'll ever eat one week from today."

"Oh, I'm sure we'll be able to eat it all. I'll share with you and Grandpa. Are you going to dress up?"

It was impossible to resist that hopeful look on her face. "I'm not going to wear a costume. But I will wear my Captain America T-shirt. How does that sound?"

"Good!" Meg took another dramatic stance and flexed her arms again.

"You'd better go take that off and get changed. We're going to the shop in a while."

Meg practically oozed stubbornness. "I'll be

careful, and I won't get grease or anything on my costume. Can I wear it? Oh please, please, please?" She folded her hands and put them below her chin while tilting her head to the side.

His adorable little drama queen. That look of hope on her face was almost enough to make him cave. "You know the rules. Only play clothes to the shop. Besides, shouldn't that costume be in the closet?" His daughter frowned. "You can wear it as much as you want to after Halloween."

Meg's arms fell to her sides, her shoulders rolled forward, and she stuck her lower lip out. "I'll bet if I had a mom, *she* would let me wear it." With that, she turned and stomped from the room.

Her comment hit Tyler in the gut with almost as much force as a punch. Why did Meg have to bring up her lack of a mother in nearly every argument now? Reece hadn't seen their daughter since Meg was three days old. Tyler had tried to talk to Meg about her sudden obsession with her mother, but Meg remained tight-lipped. He would've been angry except that it was obvious his baby girl was hurting.

Dad came in then, concern on his face. "You okay?"

Tyler grunted. "Just dealing with the Reece effect." He shook his head to clear his ex from his thoughts. "Meg wanted to wear her Halloween costume all day, and I sent her to change. She insists I dress up for next Saturday, too. You sure you don't want to go trick-or-treating with us?"

Dad smiled. "I'm positive. I'm not one for all those crowds."

Tyler wasn't normally, either. But the thought he'd hopefully see Beth made him look forward to this one. "I figured we could head over to the shop in an hour. I'd like to look at Beth's car right away and get her an estimate on when we can have it done."

"Sure." Dad gave him a knowing look. "Let me know what needs to be done, and I'll be happy to give her a call." There was no missing the teasing challenge on his face.

"I appreciate that, Dad. But I've got this one."

"I'm sure you do, son. I'll have to be around the shop when she comes to pick up her car. I'd like to catch a glimpse of the gal that's got my son moving her vehicle up on the priority list." He chuckled before dropping into the recliner and picking up the newspaper.

Tyler resisted the urge to protest, but even he could see right through it. He'd be lying if he said he wasn't looking forward to an excuse to call the pretty blonde that'd consistently occupied his thoughts.

After three hours of working in the shop, he dialed her number and waited anxiously for her to answer.

"Hello?"

"Beth? This is Tyler with Martin Mechanics. I had a chance to look at your car and wanted to update you. Is this a good time?"

"Sure. Give me a second to get somewhere I can hear you better." Her soft voice competed with noise in the background. She was probably working at the zoo. Was she stepping outside to talk?

Tyler tried to picture her, and all he could see was her sitting, relaxed, at the table near the jaguars. The image brought a smile to his face.

"Okay, I'm back. Sorry about that. How bad is it?"

Tyler relayed the news about her faulty ignition and gave her a quote on the price. "I should have it done and ready for you Wednesday afternoon." A moment of silence. "Beth? You still there?"

"Yes, I'm here. Going over figures in my mind. I've got to have my car, so I guess let's get it fixed. Could I come pick it up on Thursday? That's my day off, and it'd be a lot easier that way."

"Absolutely. Were you able to get into work okay?" He'd thought about calling her and asking if she needed a ride, but figured it was probably inappropriate seeing as how they didn't really know each other.

"My brother is letting me borrow his car until I get mine back."

"Sounds like you have a close family." He thought about her dad's birthday she mentioned last time they spoke. "How many siblings do you have?"

"I'm the youngest of five. Marian's the oldest, followed by Gwen. Then my brother, Lance, Avalon, and then me. Everyone's coming in for Dad's birthday next Saturday, although he doesn't know it yet." She chuckled. "It's going to be a madhouse."

"I bet it'll be fun." Tyler had often wondered what it would've been like to have a brother or a sister. Not that growing up as an only child was horrible. Dad was always there, even after Mom passed. But he still thought it would've been fun to get into all kinds of trouble with a sibling. He often watched Meg and wished she had someone to play with at home, too.

He and Reece had been completely clueless when they found out she was pregnant. But he would've been willing to step up and marry her. Be the kind of father his baby deserved. It was Reece who wanted to walk away, and while it had hurt then, he knew they wouldn't have lasted. The sound of Beth's voice broke him from his train of thought.

"Things are getting busy here, I'd better go. Thanks for letting me know about my car. I'll be by on Thursday. Call and let me know if it'll be later."

"I will. Have a good weekend, Beth."

"You, too."

The line went quiet and Tyler stared at the "call ended" flashing on his phone.

Dad came into the shop office then. "All right, Romeo. You ready to get back to work now?"

Tyler grabbed a rag off the table and flung it at Dad who easily dodged it.

"Yeah, yeah. I'm coming."

~

Beth rapped on the doorway of Davenport Cabinetry late Thursday morning. Lance looked up from what he was doing and waved her in. "I'll be ready to go in a minute."

"Sure, take your time." She sat on the edge of a small table and surveyed the workshop. She remembered spending time in here with Dad when he used to run it all by himself. Dad always had been proud of the work he did by hand. It'd been difficult for him to adjust to not working after his stroke.

Beth still admired the way Lance had retired from the Kitner Police Department to run Davenport Cabinetry for their father. Not every son would do such a noble thing. Then again, that was Lance. Always looking out for the people he cared about.

Thankfully, Dad was now able to come in a few times a week and help some, which was good for his spirits. Only close family could even detect the lasting effects of the stroke. Mom still felt the most comfortable, though, when he was home.

Beth knew a lot of days were hard for Dad when he was used to keeping busy all the time. The birthday party on Saturday would be a good thing for him.

Lance tossed a notebook into a drawer and stood. "Okay, let's go get that car of yours."

Beth made sure she'd stuck her checkbook into her purse after going to the bank to move money over from savings. At least Tyler hadn't called to say they needed to do more repairs than originally thought.

The realization that she was going to see him again sent her heart racing. She glanced sideways at Lance as she climbed into the passenger side of his vehicle and they pulled away from the workshop. As long as her big brother didn't detect her interest in Tyler, she'd be okay. Besides, it didn't matter anyway. It's not like she'd see Tyler again once she got her car. Disappointment left a funny taste in her mouth, and she needed something else to talk about. "How's Lexi doing?"

"She's good. Looking forward to Dad's party." He smiled at her, although there was a touch of wariness to it. "Did I tell you the adoption agency called, and we may have been matched with another birth mother?"

"No! That's awesome, Lance."

"It is. But after the last time, we don't want to tell everyone else yet."

Beth nodded. "I get it. I won't say a word, but I'll be keeping fingers crossed and praying this will be the one."

"I appreciate it." He grinned.

Lance and Lexi started going through the process to become licensed foster parents at the beginning of the year. But halfway through the classes, Lexi doubted she'd be able to take a child in only to have to say goodbye if they weren't able to adopt him or her. That's when the couple decided on domestic adoption. Against all odds, they were quickly matched with a birth mother two months later, but the whole thing fell through when she decided to keep the baby. A good outcome for both baby and birth mom, but it'd been devastating for Beth's brother and sister-in-law. The two of them would make the most amazing parents one day when they got a chance. *Please, God, bring them a baby soon.*

"Okay, the shop is ahead on the right."

"I remember seeing this place a few times. I think Tuck brought his truck by once." Tuck was Lance's best friend and Lexi's brother.

Lance parked the car and got out to follow her into the office.

A wave of nerves hit Beth, and she swallowed. Maybe Tyler wouldn't be here, and she'd run into his dad instead. but that thought sent another wave of disappointment. She had to keep it cool so that Lance, with his teasing personality, wouldn't pick up on something that wasn't even there.

A bell over the door announced their arrival. A moment later, an older gentleman walked into the office with a rag in his hands. "Welcome, folks. Can I help you?"

"I'm Beth Davenport. I'm here to pick up my car."

"Beth, of course." He wiped his hands clean and held one out. "I'm Bill Martin. I'll go tell Tyler—he left strict instructions to let him know when you'd arrived." He gave her a wink and disappeared through a side door.

Lance's eyebrows shot up. He started to open his mouth when Beth held up a hand.

"Don't start."

Clearly her defensive reaction told him more than enough. She pushed down a sigh.

Tyler came into the room then. His gaze landed on her face first with a smile before it shifted curiously to Lance. He stretched out his hand. "Tyler Martin."

Lance shook it. "Lance Davenport."

"My brother." Beth probably didn't need to clarify that.

"It's nice to meet you." Tyler tipped his head toward Beth but didn't take his eyes off the man that was equal to him in height. "Beth mentioned her brother had loaned her a vehicle. That was real nice of you."

Lance gave Tyler a genuine smile. "I'd do almost anything for my little sister." Even though Beth gave him a subtle jab with her elbow, he continued, "I appreciate that you got her car fixed so quickly."

The men spoke about the repairs for several minutes before Tyler took out a piece of paper outlining the costs of labor and materials and presented it to Beth.

She'd known what to expect but still had to force herself to not wince as she wrote a check for the amount.

Tyler handed her a receipt. "The car's around the side. I'll meet you out there."

Lance and Beth went through the front door. They'd barely stepped outside when he tossed her a grin. "So how long have you two known each other?"

"It's not like that," she hissed in a whisper.

"Maybe not as far as you're concerned. But he clearly has a thing for you."

Beth snagged his arm to stop him. "Not a word to the rest of the family, Lance, or I swear..."

His face split into a big grin. "Your secret's safe with me. At least for now." He winked at her. "You should bring him to Dad's birthday party."

"That's not going to happen." She lowered her voice to a fierce whisper. "I doubt I'll see him after today. The last thing I need is for everyone to bother me about something that's a non-issue." Her expression softened, and she gave Lance the pleading look that'd worked on him since they were young. Well, most of the time, anyway.

Lance put a hand over his heart. "I promise."

Beth mouthed a silent, "Thank you," and led the way around the building to where her car waited. The engine was running, and Tyler stood holding the door open.

"Thank you again for fixing my car, I appreciate it."

"Not a problem. It's what we do. Hopefully it won't give you any more trouble." He smiled, his gaze resting on her a few extra moments. He turned his attention to Lance and shook his hand again. "It was nice to meet you. If you have any need for a mechanic, I hope you'll consider us. What kind of business are you in?"

"I run my father's carpentry place now. Before that, I was an officer for the KPD for years. Still have a good buddy there."

Tyler's eyes widened slightly, and Beth covered a

smile by sliding into the driver's seat. Lance liked to drop that bit of information when he was protecting his family. The truth of the matter was he still went to the gun range and worked out regularly. He could get back on the force anytime he wanted to. He seemed content to work at their dad's shop, though. She figured Lexi appreciated not having to worry as much about him that way, too.

Lance leaned down to speak with her. "Be safe, Beth. I'll see you on Saturday."

"Thanks again. I appreciate you."

Her brother waved and went back to the front parking lot and his car.

Beth raised her eyes to find Tyler watching her, one side of his mouth quirked up in a smile. "I'm bringing Meg to the zoo on Saturday morning. We'll keep an eye out for you."

"What's she dressing up as?"

"Wonder Woman. Possibly with a princess tiara thrown in." He laughed.

"My kind of girl. I'll see if I can spot her, too."

Tyler closed the door for her. Beth pulled through the parking spot and made herself not look in the rearview mirror as she drove away.

Only then did she release the shaky breath she'd been holding. So much for her attempt to ignore the way Tyler's presence made her pulse skitter. It was impossible to deny how happy she was at the prospect of seeing him again in a couple of days.

Chapter Five

Tyler planned to arrive at the zoo soon after ten when trick-or-treating started. He was surprised to see the long line of families waiting at the entrance. It was clear, however, that the staff at the zoo had this event down to a science. He and Meg got through the line quickly and were soon handed a map of the stations offering treats, then turned loose inside the zoo.

Meg was excited and could hardly stand still. She was bouncing on one foot, hopping up and down, or holding Tyler's hand and trying to pull him one way then another. He stopped her, handed the red bag to her, and crouched down to her eye level. "You are to stay right by me at all times. It's busy here and it'd be easy for you to get lost. Again. Do you understand?"

Her eyes widened as she remembered the turmoil of their last zoo visit. "Yes, Daddy. I'll make sure I stay next to you." She clung to the bag with her right hand and then held his hand with her other. "I can't wait to get some candy. And see the animals. I hope we can see Miss Beth again, too. What if she got sick and couldn't be here?"

Tyler smiled at his enthusiastic young daughter. "She said she'd be near the giraffes. I guess we'll find out when we get there. Are you ready to get started?"

She bobbed her head.

They decided on the path closest to the giraffes first. Since Beth said she had to leave early to go to a birthday party, Tyler didn't want to chance missing her. As they progressed from station to station, Meg received more candy than she'd know what to do with. Everywhere he looked, there was a sea of kids dressed up like super heroes and princesses. The zoo staff were dressed up as well, and he wondered what costume Beth went with.

A colorful sign indicated they were nearing the giraffe exhibit. He scanned the crowd at the station ahead, and it was a full minute before he realized the woman he was staring at was Beth.

She wore a blue medieval-style dress that flowed in waves past her ankles to the ground. The neck scooped down a bit while gold stitching along the hems made the dress look like something a royal would wear. The shade of blue made her eyes appear almost electric.

As he and Meg waited in a line that slowly got closer to Beth, he thought this was the first time he'd seen her with her hair down. Instead of being pulled into a pony tail or braided, it flowed down her back like a blonde waterfall. A little was pulled into a clip with only a few strands escaping to hang around her face.

Stunning.

When they reached the front of the line, Beth's face lit up as she smiled at them. "Hey, you two. I'm glad you made it." She knelt to give Meg her choice of lollipops. "You look amazing, Wonder Woman. If I need to be rescued, can I call you?"

Meg beamed. "You bet! I'll save you! Daddy's Captain America. He can save you too." Her face got serious. "If you need to be carried out of a burning building or something, you'd better call him. I don't think I can lift you." She looked down into her bag and admired the ridiculously large candy stash inside, oblivious to the chuckles from the adults around her. "I wish you could go trick-or-treating with us. That would be fun."

Tyler helped Meg shift to the side so that people could get some candy and go past them. He wasn't in a hurry to leave Beth and Meg didn't seem to be, either.

"So do I, sweetie. But if I leave, none of these kids will get lollipops." Beth gave Tyler a wink which made his heart flip flop in his chest. "Don't you want to go get some more candy?"

Meg frowned. "I have lots. If I eat too much, my teeth will rot right out of my head."

Tyler chuckled. At least he knew his daughter listened to him occasionally.

Humor sparked in Beth's eyes. "If you and your daddy aren't in a hurry to leave, would you like to help me hand out candy to the other kids?"

"Oh, yes!" Meg swung around fast enough to hit Tyler in the leg with her treat bag. "Can we, Daddy? Please?"

Tyler wasn't about to say no to spending more time with Beth, even if his common sense insisted he should insist they continue on their way. "For a little while."

"Yippee!" Meg shoved her candy bag into Tyler's arms and turned to help Beth.

Tyler would've helped as well, but the two ladies seemed to have it covered. Instead, he set his stuff on a rock behind the station and took several pictures with his phone. He sent one to Dad along with a text explaining what Meg was doing.

Beth stepped back a bit as Meg all but took over handing the candy out. "Your daughter is a natural."

"That's because she's a people person." Tyler smiled at his little girl. "I admire that about her. I wasn't nearly as outgoing when I was a kid."

"Me, either." Beth smoothed her skirt out and shuffled to one side, tripping over something. One hand shot out to steady herself, landing against his chest.

Without thinking, he put his own hand over hers, effectively trapping it between his palm and his pounding heart. She lifted her head, giving him the perfect opportunity to study those gorgeous eyes of hers. He nearly complimented her on how pretty she was and swapped out his words at the last moment. "Your dress is beautiful. You don't usually see something that detailed being sold as a Halloween costume."

She seemed flustered as she regained her footing and stepped back. Tyler instantly missed the warmth of her hand against his skin.

"My family goes to Renaissance festivals. This is one of the dresses I wear."

"One of them?"

Pink cheeks morphed into red. "I have another in green and one in pink. The key to wearing a fancy dress like this is the footwear." She lifted her skirt high enough to reveal a pair of gray sneakers and laughed.

Tyler imagined seeing her in a pink dress to

match her cheeks and wished he could witness such beauty in person. "Good thinking on the shoes. I've never been to one of those festivals, but they sound like fun."

"Oh, they are a blast." She told him about the last one her family had gone to, pausing here and there to help Meg or to accept a new bag of candy from a coworker. "If you ever have an opportunity to go to one, you should. The food alone is reason enough."

Her animation completely enthralled him. He found himself hoping he could go with her next year until he grasped exactly what that would mean. They'd only had a handful of conversations and here he was already considering future activities with her. Tyler watched his daughter and frowned as everything that happened between him and his ex resurfaced, along with a storm of conflicting emotions.

Meg looked up into Beth's face and smiled with adoration. She was becoming attached to her own hero, and the thought scared Tyler. She didn't even remember Reece, yet the woman had left permanent scars on their daughter's heart. How much more damage could be caused by someone Meg got attached to?

He cleared his throat. "You know, we should probably be getting back. Grandpa's holding down the shop for me, kiddo. We need to let him go to lunch." Meg stuck her lip out and started to pout but he stopped her. "No, ma'am. You've had a lot of fun and even got to help Beth. I don't want to hear any complaints. Understand?"

"Yes, sir." She turned to Beth. "Thank you for letting me help you."

"You're welcome. I'm not sure I could've handed

all that candy out if you hadn't been here to help me."

Beth's praise had Meg standing taller, a proud look on her face.

Tyler took her hand in his, handed her the candy bag again, and paused. "I hope your dad's birthday party goes well this afternoon."

"Thank you. I'm sure it will. You two have a lovely rest of your weekend." Beth waved and then turned to hand more candy out to the growing crowds. She wasn't kidding when she said it only got busier as the day went on.

Tyler was feeling claustrophobic by the time they got back to his car. He helped Meg into her booster seat.

"That was fun, Daddy. Do you think we can go back and see Beth tomorrow?"

"I don't think so. She doesn't work at the zoo on Sundays."

"I hope we get to see her again soon."

Tyler affectionately rubbed the top of her head. "Yeah, me, too."

~

"Surprise!"

Beth grinned as Dad's face transformed from shocked to astounded to pleased. Mom had insisted they needed a few things at the store and kept Dad out of the house long enough for everyone to arrive and set the place up with decorations and food. It was clear the last thing he expected to come home to was his entire family.

Grandkids threw themselves at him for hugs before the rest of them got a chance. Mom swooped right in and took the bundle of blue from Gwen's arms. "Let me see my newest grandson."

Avalon gave Gwen a hug. "I'm glad you three could make it! I know it's not easy driving with a baby."

"You know, Cade did a lot better than I thought he would. We only had to stop to feed him twice and change him, then he slept the rest of the time. Not bad for five and a half hours. Of course, he'll probably be up all night now."

"If that's the case, I'm sure Mom won't mind helping out."

Gwen, Zane, and the baby were staying at Mom and Dad's house tonight. Marian and her family of six planned to spend the night with Lance and Lexi. While Avalon and Beth both would've been happy to have someone stay with them, their smaller places didn't leave a lot of room for guests.

They laughed as poor Lorelei tried to chase around after her three much older cousins. At least young Samuel was only five months older than her, so she wouldn't be left behind completely. It was amazing how much the family had grown over the last ten years. What would it look like in another decade?

Beth would probably still be the only single sibling, she thought wryly. When everything happened with Carl, she'd been determined to be the doting aunt who did everything with her nieces and nephews and didn't need to have kids of her own.

Now, as she watched all of them play, she couldn't get young Meg out of her head. The girl would fit right in with the others. She suddenly pictured herself standing hand-in-hand with Tyler, and the image threw her for a loop. What on earth was she thinking? The guy had fixed her car and visited with her at the zoo. That she was even entertaining any more than that was absurd.

Gwen moved to accept her infant son and took him for a diaper change. Lance wandered over and gave Beth a gentle nudge in the shoulder. "How you doing? Seen any mechanics lately?"

Beth pivoted and gave him a lame punch to the stomach. He lifted both hands in surrender as he laughed. "You promised you wouldn't say a word."

"And I keep my promises. Doesn't mean I can't tease in the process, does it?"

"Well, it'd be nice if that was included in the deal." She raised an eyebrow at him and folded her arms against her chest. "Besides, it seems we both have things we're trying to keep on the downlow. Any news?"

Lance's face grew serious. "We're meeting with the birth mother a week from Thursday. Keep us in your prayers, huh?"

"Will do, big brother. Let me know how it goes when you're up to it, okay?" Beth spotted Lexi on the far side of the room. Her sister-in-law could have allowed a hysterectomy for cervical cancer and her inability to have children of her own make her bitter. Instead, she delighted in the attention of her nieces and nephews. Lexi was truly an inspiration. Lorelei ran over with a book and settled into Lexi's lap, her little thumb going into her mouth as Lexi began to read. It didn't look like there was anywhere else Lexi would rather be. She turned to find Lance watching her, too.

"I need this one to go through, Beth. Lexi wants kids more than anything. All her time is spent with her nieces and nephews, helping kids at the pediatrician's office, or volunteering to hold the babies in the NICU.

She deserves to rock her own one day." His voice sounded rough, and he cleared his throat.

"So do you, Lance." Beth wrapped her arms around his and gave it a squeeze. "We're all praying. It's going to happen."

He nodded once.

Mom came into the room and clapped her hands. "Okay, everyone! Dinner will be ready soon. Why don't we let the birthday boy open his presents while we wait?"

The kids cheered and raced each other for a spot on the floor at their grandfather's feet.

Dad looked around the room from his spot on the couch and brushed a tear from his eye. "Having you all here at one time is the best present I could've ever asked for."

Beth sniffed and blinked back her own tears. Dad was right. Family was everything.

Would it be worth the risk to open herself up to the possibility of having a family of her own one day?

Chapter Six

Tyler watched as Meg handed a tool to Dad. Then she stood next to him, her hands on her hips. With her head titled to one side, she shook it thoughtfully. "I don't know, Grandpa. I think it might be the battery."

Tyler stifled a laugh and admired the way Dad corrected her with a straight face.

"I don't know about that, sweetie. I'm pretty sure it's the fuel injector. Why don't we give that a look?"

"Okay." She dragged her step stool closer to the car allowing her to see inside the hood.

Tyler didn't think there was anything much cuter than the sight of his daughter, grease smudges on her cheeks and overalls, helping her grandfather work on a car. Who knows? Maybe she'd grow up to be a mechanic like them? He rather doubted it, though, since Meg had insisted for the last two years that she was going to work at a zoo.

With that, his thoughts settled on Beth. It'd been a week since he saw her when he took Meg trick-or-treating. He'd been tempted to call her or drop by the zoo every day. Would she welcome his visits, or would he end up with a restraining order? The thought might have amused him if he weren't in such a quandary over what he should do.

"Would you ask the woman out?"

Tyler blinked, bringing Dad into focus. "What?" Apparently, Meg had gotten bored at some point and was now playing with puzzles in the small office. How long had he been consumed with his thoughts?

"Beth. Ask her out. I haven't seen you this distracted about a woman in years."

Great. He thought he'd been doing okay keeping his thoughts to himself. So much for that. "She hasn't given me any encouragement. What if she says no?"

"Then come up with an outing. Take Meg with you." He nodded toward the chair where Meg was playing with a toy she'd brought. "No one can resist her." He chuckled and went back to work.

Maybe Dad was right. Beth mentioned she was off work on Thursdays. A plan started to form. He found Beth's number, stepped outside, and dialed it. She answered on the third ring. "Hello?"

"Hi, Beth. This is Tyler. How are you doing today?"

"Hi! I'm good, thanks. You caught me in between tours." Her soft voice washed over him and eased the worry he'd felt before calling. "How's your week going?"

"It's going well." He paused. "Meg and I have thought about changing our weekly after school ice cream to Thursdays. We were wondering if you'd like to join us this week." He held his breath. *Come on, Beth.* He hadn't asked a woman out in years. Not since

Reece. He couldn't believe how vulnerable this made him feel.

"I don't know. I mean, I appreciate the offer. And you know how much fun I have with the two of you." She paused. "I'm not ready to date anyone, Tyler. I had a bad breakup. I'm not sure I'm ready to put myself out there like that again."

There was something about her voice that suggested there was more to her story.

"Getting ice cream with a six-year-old is a date?" Okay, he was reaching, and probably sounding desperate.

Her chuckle barely came across the line. "Just ice cream, huh?"

"Just ice cream."

More silence. "I'd like that."

Tyler gave a silent arm pump and grinned. He gave her the information about where to meet and what time. "Meg and I look forward to it."

"So do I. Oh, I'd better run. Things are getting crazy around here. See you on Thursday."

"See you then." Tyler hung up and slid his phone into his back pocket. Thursday was now officially the highlight of his week. And if he kept focused on the fact that this wasn't a date, it made it a lot easier to ignore the nervous energy coursing through his veins.

~

Beth rubbed her damp palms on her jeans. How was it possible that meeting someone for ice cream could make her this nervous? She tried to laugh at herself, but it didn't work. She should've told Tyler no or said she had other plans. Something. But mixed in with the nerves and worry was anticipation. It was hard to resist the opportunity to see him again when she hadn't thought she would.

She entered the ice cream shop and spotted Tyler and Meg at a corner table. The moment Meg saw her, she hopped down from her chair and ran across the dining room. "Beth!"

"Hey, Meg!" Beth stooped to give the girl a hug. "I'm glad to see you again. Don't tell me you like ice cream."

"I love it! Especially strawberry. Have you ever had strawberry ice cream? It's the best with chocolate syrup and M&Ms on top." Meg's eyes held such excitement it was impossible for some of it to not rub off on Beth.

"Wow, that sounds good. I can't say I've had that combination."

"So what flavor is your favorite?" Tyler's deep voice spoke from nearby. She hadn't noticed him walk up.

Beth stood again, surprised that Meg held onto her hand while reaching over for her daddy's as well. Beth looked at the ice cream choices. "You know, that's a difficult question. Are there bad flavors of ice cream?"

Tyler laughed, the sound rolling over her and causing a jolt of electricity to race down her spine. "Now that's what I'm talking about. Although I've never been a fan of pistachio. I don't hate it, but it's not a favorite." He tipped his head toward the counter. "Shall we?"

Beth ordered a waffle cone with a scoop of blueberry cheesecake. Her mouth watered thinking about it. Before she could pay for her ice cream, Tyler had paid for all three of them.

They went out the back door and made their way to a picnic table outside. Several children were running and playing on the fenced-in playground.

Beth chuckled when Meg scooped up a huge spoonful of ice cream sundae and somehow managed to fit the whole thing in her mouth.

"Smaller bites, girl." Tyler gave his daughter a firm look that she seemed to ignore. He raised an eyebrow at Beth before taking a bite of his own dark chocolate ice cream cone. "Watch this kid of mine. She'll finish that ice cream in record time and then somehow still run around. If I did that, I'd get sick."

"I probably would, too." Beth grinned and relished the way her ice cream melted in her mouth. She hadn't had blueberry cheesecake in forever. She probably liked the ice cream even better than the actual cake. "I would've bought my own cone."

"This one's on me. You can buy your own next time." He winked at her.

What was that supposed to mean? That he hoped she'd meet them for ice cream again? Was he asking her to? She wished she knew. Since she said she didn't date, he was probably only teasing. The thought led to an unexpected wave of disappointment.

They ate in comfortable conversation until Meg finished her ice cream and went to play. The little girl glanced back with a wave.

"She's beautiful, you know." Beth waved at Meg. "She looks a lot like you."

"I appreciate that. She's something else." He smiled tenderly and then laughed when Meg went down the slide with her arms up and a whoop. He looked down at the napkin on the table and then back up at Beth. "You mentioned on the phone that you don't date. Ever? Or is this a temporary ban?"

His sparkling eyes and smile managed to elicit a grin from her. "Let's just say my last relationship has made me determined to keep the past from repeating." Even though she'd carefully thought out her response, it still sounded harsh. "Sorry. It's nothing against you."

"So you're telling me some guy ruined it for the rest of us?"

When he put it that way... She gave a noncommittal shrug. She didn't want to dive into what happened with Carl. It was time to deflect the conversation. "If you don't mind my asking, what happened to Meg's mother?"

The moment the words were out, she saw the same panic in his eyes that she'd felt herself a moment ago. "I'm sorry. I wasn't trying to pry."

"No, it's okay." Tyler watched Meg for a moment. He seemed to struggle with whether to say more or change the subject. "Reece and I went out in high school for a couple of years, and we both figured we'd get married at some point after we graduated. That didn't last long, though. We broke up a month into our freshman year of college. A few weeks later, she found out she was pregnant with Meg." He ran one hand through his hair and sighed. "It changed everything. Reece wasn't even sure she wanted to keep the baby, but I promised I'd raise her. Reece jumped at the chance, signed over her rights not long after Meg was born, and walked away."

"Wow. I'm sorry." Beth didn't know what kind of story she'd expected, but this sure wasn't it. She couldn't imagine walking away from her own baby, but then it was clear she didn't know all the details. Beth shook her head. "I'm sure that had to be hard for you."

"It was horrible, and we were both way too young to handle the situation with as much maturity as we could have. But I had Meg." He smiled sweetly as he watched his daughter play. "Everything with her made it worthwhile." He polished off the last of his cone and wiped his hands on the napkin. He stared at the chain link fence that surrounded the park, or maybe it was at something he could see beyond it. Beth sure didn't have any sage advice to offer him.

Tyler finally roused himself from his thoughts and focused on Beth. "I'm sorry, that's way more than you ever wanted to know, right?"

Beth shrugged. "We've all got things in our past that continue to affect us now. Some of them are a lot harder to shake than others." She held his gaze. It seemed they'd both been through past relationships that had left their own scars.

"Daddy!"

Meg's call got their attention. She'd fallen and scraped her knee on the pavement. With tears streaming down her face, Tyler kissed her knee and then pulled a bandage out of his wallet to patch it up. An expert. Meg laid her head on his shoulder and let out a little sigh.

"Are you getting tired, baby?" She nodded. "Maybe we should get you home."

Beth had finished her ice cream and picked up all the trash to throw away. "I had a lot of fun. Thank you both for inviting me to join you."

Meg lifted her head and gave Beth a hopeful look. "Are you coming to my birthday party?"

"I didn't know you had a birthday coming up soon. You'll be seven, right?"

"Yep!" Even though there were remnants of tears in the corners of her eyes, Meg grinned, the fall forgotten. "I'm going to have a super hero cake and balloons. And I hope I get a ballet dress!"

The shift from super heroes to ballet dress made Beth pause.

Tyler tossed her an apologetic look. "Her birthday isn't until the second week of December. But she's been planning it since January."

Beth smiled at Meg. "There's nothing wrong with being organized, is there?"

Meg shook her head, hair getting in her face. "So, will you come?"

Beth looked from her to Tyler and back. What was she supposed to say? "Oh, I bet you'll have plans with your family."

That's when Meg's happy face turned into a sad frown. "Oh, yes. Daddy and Grandpa will be there and some of my friends. But I *really* want you to come, too. Please?"

Tyler gave his daughter a firm look. "It's too early to make plans like that. We'll talk about your birthday party after Thanksgiving. Okay?"

"Okay," Meg agreed, although her voice didn't sound overly pleased. She scrambled down from her dad's arms and threw her own around Beth. "I'll miss you. I hope we can have ice cream again soon. Next time, you'll have to try a sundae like me."

"I'm going to miss you, too. You have a great rest of your week, okay?"

They walked together to the parking lot where Tyler helped Meg inside his vehicle and gave Beth a final wave.

All the way home, Beth couldn't fight against the

smile that almost made her cheeks ache. She checked the time on the console. Lance and Lexi had a meeting scheduled with the birth mother this morning. Beth almost went home like she'd planned, but instead stopped by Davenport Cabinetry. She found Lance inside sanding down some shelves.

He looked up and smiled. "Hey, Beth."

"Hey yourself. I was in the neighborhood and thought I'd come say hi to my favorite brother." She nodded toward the shelves. "Looks like you're staying busy."

"Things pick up this time of the year. People are turning in a lot of orders for furniture they're giving as Christmas gifts. Although these are for Daisy. Apparently, several of the shelves in one of her pantries are sagging beyond use. The dimension is so odd, she needed some cut to fit."

"It's nice of you to do that." Beth sat down and rested her chin in one hand. "How'd the meeting go this morning?"

Lance frowned. "Honestly? I wish I knew. The birth mom—Kate—seemed nice. But she's also unsure. I don't know if she's hesitant about adoption in general or if it's us specifically. We're back in a holding pattern, waiting to hear from the agency. Poor Lex is on the edge of her seat; she's nervous about this one. We were talking about it last night, and even if the birth mother does choose us, I think we're going to keep it quiet until the baby's in our arms."

Beth made a cross over her heart with one finger. "I promise I won't say a thing to anyone. I'm praying, though. And if you need someone to talk to, you know I'm here."

"I appreciate it." Lance finished the shelf he was

working on and set it down. "How are things going with your mechanic?"

She made a face. "I don't know. I met him and Meg for ice cream a little while ago. It's weird because, when we're all together, everything feels natural. But when I'm not around him, I second guess everything. We both have a lot of relationship baggage that's weighing us down."

Her family knew what had happened with Carl. Lance, especially, had been her rock during that time. They'd gotten a lot closer, and he was one of the few people she talked to about men even now. "I thought I knew Carl after two years, and he proved me wrong. I don't know that I'm ready to put myself out there for someone I've only known for a month."

Lance put everything down and pulled a chair near Beth's. "I get what you're saying, and I couldn't agree with you more. But take it from someone who wasted way too much time. How many years could Lexi and I have been together if I'd told her how I felt from the beginning?"

He had a point. Lance and Lexi had known each other most of their lives. Lance saw her often when he'd go over to Tuck's house growing up. Beth was convinced Lance had probably been in love with her for almost as long. But it took Lexi's cancer diagnosis to make him understand how short life could be and finally act on his feelings.

She sighed. "I know. It's much easier said than done, though."

"That's the truth. But the thing is, you don't know unless you try." He shrugged and then winked. "I'm not saying you should up and marry the guy tomorrow. Like you said, you don't know each other well, but it doesn't hurt to give it a chance and see how well you two get along. Regardless, you can't allow fear to make that decision for you. Not all of us men are bad guys, you know?"

She winced as his comment hit the nail on the head. "I appreciate the sage advice, older brother of mine."

He slapped his legs with his hands and stood up. "Okay, you'd better get out of my hair so I can get this finished up and get home early. If the agency doesn't call, Lexi's going to be a worried mess tonight."

Beth stood, too, and gave him a hug. "I'll be praying. Thanks again, Lance. I'll see you guys again soon. Call me if you need anything."

She headed home, made a sandwich for dinner, and sat in front of her laptop. After taking in a deep breath, she opened her e-mail, fully expecting mostly junk like usual. The name of her illustrator jumped off the screen. Beth pushed her plate back and opened the e-mail hurriedly. All the illustrations for her book were attached, including the cover they'd talked about, and they surpassed her expectations. With tears in her eyes, she looked through each of them several times. Perfect.

The realization that this meant she could finally put the book together and publish it was almost overwhelming. She spent the rest of her evening working on formatting, image placement, and a million other things.

When everything was ready, she submitted it for review with the printing company. If it was approved, she'd be able to order a proof of the book. She couldn't wait to hold a copy in her hands and wished that she hadn't let nerves and uncertainty stand in the way of putting her book together sooner.

She leaned back in her chair and thought about what Lance said earlier. What if he was right? Was she letting her past with Carl become a roadblock to her future?

Chapter Seven

Tyler frowned at his reflection in the mirror. The oil smudges on his forehead and right cheek spoke of a particularly grueling day. It made Tuesday feel like a second Monday.

Dad clapped him on the shoulder. "You alright, son?"

"Yeah, just tired. I think Meg woke up four times last night for various reasons." He yawned. "I hope she sleeps better tonight."

Dad covered a yawn of his own. "I hear ya. I felt bad for the both of you. But if we can get these two cars finished up, I think tomorrow's going to be a lighter day."

"I sure hope so." He tilted his head toward the fridge in the corner of the small breakroom. "I'm going to grab a bottle of water. Do you want one?"

"Sure."

"All right. I'll be back out to help you in a sec."

Tyler pulled the last two bottles of cold water out of the fridge. Knowing they'd want more later, he opened a new case and placed those bottles in the fridge to chill. He'd barely closed the door when his phone beeped with a text. He was surprised to see Beth's name.

"I was thinking about you and Meg. How's her knee doing?"

The thought that he'd entered her mind long enough to inspire her to send a text made him smile. He texted back. "It's fine. She didn't even notice it by the time we got home. We're both dragging today, though. She kept waking up last night, and I wondered if her allergies were kicking in."

Beth responded in moments. "It may be something going around. My sister said the same thing about my niece. Hopefully tonight will be better."

"I sure hope so."

Truthfully, he'd been thinking about Beth since he saw her at the ice cream shop. She'd made it clear she didn't date, but he had a feeling there was more to her story. Even though he respected her decision, the thought of not seeing her again bothered him.

He decided to go with his gut and started to text before he changed his mind. "I had fun the other day. I'd like to do that again. Can I bring you lunch tomorrow?"

He hit send and hoped it wasn't too forward. What if she said no? What if she decided he hadn't listened to her at all when they were talking and regretted texting him in the first place? Tyler half wished he could take the text back.

But what if she said yes? It was that minute possibility that kept him watching his phone. Fifteen minutes later, he decided the worst response was getting none at all. He tried to put it out of his mind as he and his dad worked to get the cars finished up. The more they did before Tyler left to pick up Meg from school, the better off they'd be.

Another half hour later, a text came in. Tyler wiped as much grease from his hands off on his pants before swiping the screen to read it.

"What if we meet as two friends and eat lunch together? I'll have mine here, and if you'd like to bring yours, you're more than welcome. I get lunch at twelve thirty."

Friends, huh? Well, it was a start, and at least she hadn't said no. After going through everything with Reece, the thought of getting close to anyone else was scary. Yet, for a reason he couldn't quite explain, he really wanted a proper date with Beth. If she was even half as reluctant as he on the prospect of dating again, it probably wouldn't be easy. He responded to the text. "Sounds good. Same place I found you the first time?"

"Yep."

"I'll be there. See you tomorrow." Tyler gave his phone a satisfied shove into his pocket and went back to work. One way or another, these cars were going to be done by tonight so he'd be free to spend lunch with Beth.

~

Tyler was glad he'd grabbed his jacket before going into the zoo. It was chilly after a cold front hit late last night with rain predicted for the next few days. He took in the cloudy sky, glad that it didn't look like rain anytime soon. That was good because he didn't want anything canceling his lunch with Beth.

Dad teased him all morning about his "date"

even though Tyler had assured him it wasn't one. Truthfully, he was kind of considering it a date himself. What mattered, though, was that Beth did not since she'd made it clear yesterday they were meeting as friends only.

He found her at the same table as the day he'd come to thank her for finding Meg. This time, she sat in a chair facing his direction. The moment she spotted him, a smile graced her face as she waved. She wore a pair of dark jeans and a purple zoo T-shirt over a black, long-sleeved shirt. A canvas bag sat on the ground next to her feet. She kicked it over when she stood, then bent to right it again. She reached for the ponytail that held her hair together at the back of her head and wound some strands around her finger.

Was it only Tyler, or did she seem flustered? Was it a good fluster, or a bad one? He sought out her eyes and found genuine pleasure at seeing him again. Good, the feeling was mutual. "Hi! How's your day been so far?"

"Not bad. I survived a field trip this morning and consider that a win." Beth sat back down, and Tyler followed suit, choosing a chair next to hers instead of across the table.

"When did you start giving field trips?"

"Yesterday was my first." She flashed a big smile. "I'm hoping to help out with the summer camps next year, and this is a great step in that direction."

"In that case, congratulations." Tyler thoroughly enjoyed the happy look on her face. He held up the bag he'd brought. "Cheeseburger and fries." He pointed to the popular chain restaurant's logo. "I made it myself."

Beth laughed, the sound washing over Tyler.

"Don't feel bad. I brought cold pizza and a

soda." She unpacked her own lunch. "You know, I should've thought to suggest we meet out at the park. It's close by and then you wouldn't have had to pay to come into the zoo. I'm sorry I didn't think of it before." She reached for her bag. "I can reimburse you for the ticket."

Tyler held up a hand to stop her. "Don't worry about it. I bought a pass for the next year." She looked at him in surprise, a question in her gaze. "I thought I might be coming by more often than normal, and a family pass seemed to be the most economical choice." He flashed her a smile, satisfied to see pink warm her cheeks.

"How are Meg and your dad?"

"They're good. We're all looking forward to fall break. I think Meg needs some time off from school." Originally, he'd hoped a break would help with some of her attitude issues. Now that he thought about it, though, the attitude Meg had been carrying around with her all but disappeared after they met Beth for ice cream. He could only hope the trend would continue. Beth seemed concerned by his silence but held her tongue. He appreciated it, but there was also something about her that made him want to share about things he didn't normally tell anyone else but Dad. "Meg's been throwing a lot of fits lately. She's an emotional storm these days. I'm not real sure what to do with her sometimes."

Beth studied him a moment. "Does it help to know that my oldest sister has said the same about all of her kids at that age?"

A small laugh escaped him. "Yeah, actually it does. I've got parenting books, and Dad pitches in, but he never raised a girl, either. There have been many times when it would've been great to have my mom's take on all this."

She gave her head a shake, her golden ponytail moving along with it. "Raising girls compared to boys can be very different. But at the end of the day, it's about balancing discipline and encouragement. You have to tailor how you approach both depending on the child."

Tyler blinked at her. "I'm impressed."

"Don't be. I'm mostly regurgitating all I've heard from my own parents and my sisters. No practical experience to share." She looked thoughtful. "Honestly, Meg seems to adore you. From what everyone frequently tells me, parenting isn't easy, but from an outsider looking in, it seems you're doing a great job."

He'd been worrying about Meg a lot lately, and while most of that didn't magically disappear, Beth's soothing words seemed to shrink some of those problems. He scratched his chin through his beard and marveled at how she'd known what he'd needed to hear. "I appreciate that. Thank you." He paused. "Okay, enough about my parenting challenges. What are you doing for Thanksgiving?"

"It'll be a big family affair. Not everyone will be there, but those of us in the area will go to my parents' house for dinner."

There was something in her voice that hinted she might not be too happy about the arrangement. "And you'd rather not go?"

"It's not that." She took a bite of her pizza and chewed thoughtfully. "I'm the youngest. My brother and sisters are all married, so everyone focuses their matchmaking abilities on me, and it's not something I want to deal with this year." She shrugged as if it were no big deal and that was the end to the situation.

"You know, if you let me take you out on an official date, you'd at least have something to tell them. Maybe it would get them off your back a little." He intended it to be more of a joke with a half-hope she'd agree. He hadn't anticipated the flash of uncertainty that bordered on desperation in her eyes.

Tyler took a long draw from his cold bottle of water as he considered his next words. "I know you're not dating, but a guy can't help wondering if it's just him." He was mostly joking, though he was curious, and gave her a humorous smile.

Beth picked at the crust of her pizza, putting a tiny piece on her tongue. She shrugged and didn't quite meet his eyes. "My last relationship was rough. Carl, he…" She paused. "It was a bad break up, and I'm afraid it's made me a little jaded about dating again in general." Beth raised her gaze to his, her eyes filled with equal parts determination and insecurity.

It was the latter part that pulled at Tyler's heartstrings. What had her ex done to cause her to lose self-confidence like this? Anger replaced his curiosity, and he pushed it down to keep it from overflowing into his actions and words. "I think I've proven I'm less than stellar when it comes to my past relationships, too." That got a little smile from her. "I haven't dated since Reece. I guess I hadn't wanted to risk it. Until now." That got her complete attention, and there was no missing the surprise on her face. "I'd like to get to know you better, Beth, but only if that's something you'd like, too." There, he'd said it.

Beth's eyes widened. She twirled some of her hair around a finger a moment before dropping it. "I…"

She swallowed. "I'd like to get to know you better, too."

Her words lifted the virtual brick right off his chest. He grinned. "I'm glad. What if I come back and meet you for lunch again on Friday?"

Beth tried to keep back a smile but failed miserably. "You don't waste any time, do you?"

"I see no reason why I should." He wadded up his food wrappers and put them back in the bag. "Is that a yes?"

"I can't." She fixed him with a serious look before allowing a small smile to escape. "I'm supposed to trade lunches with Monique, and we have a staff meeting that day too. I have no idea when I'll actually be eating, or if I'll have the full hour." She paused. "What about Monday?"

"Monday works. Besides, it'll give me a few days to convince you to let me buy your lunch and bring it along."

She hiked an eyebrow but didn't argue. He decided to take that as a yes and run with it. Unfortunately, their time together ended much sooner than he would've liked. He had to leave forty minutes in to give him enough time to get to the car and get back to work. He said goodbye to Beth and reluctantly left her at the table.

He thought about her all the way back to his car. He realized that the only time he'd seen her hair down was at the zoo's Halloween event. Otherwise she kept it pulled back in a ponytail or braided down her back. He made a mental note to ask her about it someday, although their first official date was probably a little too soon for that.

He grinned. He, Tyler Martin, had a date on

Monday with a gorgeous woman. Who would've thought it?

Chapter Eight

W hat are you smiling about?" Monique gave Beth a mischievous look on Monday morning. "I don't suppose it has to do with the guy who bought a family pass last week."

Beth shrugged but couldn't keep the grin off her face. "Maybe."

"Uh-huh." A customer came in, and Monique had no choice but to drop the subject, but it was clear from the look on her face that she wasn't going to forget.

Beth hadn't told anyone about her lunch date with Tyler today. She went through the rest of last week and the weekend half hoping he would call or text to cancel. At least then she wouldn't have to deal with the mix of emotions that assailed her every time she thought about him. Beth couldn't wait to see him again, yet the thought of allowing herself to get too attached to him, not to mention Meg, was more than scary.

But Tyler didn't cancel. In fact, he called once over the weekend just to see how she was doing and to find out what her favorite foods were. He wouldn't tell her what he was bringing for lunch, but promised she'd like it.

She'd also heard from Lance yesterday. The birth mother chose him and Lexi to be the adoptive parents of her unborn baby. Beth wanted to shout her excitement from the rooftop, but after the last match fell apart, she more than understood their reasons for wanting to keep quiet. This baby was due the first week of January. Beth prayed fervently that her brother and sweet sister-in-law would be holding him or her in their arms for the new year.

Monique finished with her customer and took the few moments of reprieve to lean against the counter closest to Beth. "Spill."

Beth did her best to shrug nonchalantly. "Tyler's bringing lunch by today. We're going to eat together. It's no big deal."

"No big deal?" Monique fixed her with a look that would've made most people take a step back. "You're either clueless or messing with me."

Beth chuckled but said nothing else.

Monique shook her head and focused on her work. "Fine. But I expect a report when you get back."

A couple of hours later, Beth collected her bag and headed out of the gift shop and into the bright, but cool, November sun. She hadn't taken a handful of steps when she heard someone jogging up behind her.

Tyler reached her side and slowed again. "I was going to meet you at the gift shop and walk you to lunch. I'll have to remember to get here a little earlier next time."

His friendly smile made Beth's heart soar. "When it's my time for lunch, I take it seriously."

"Because you're hungry, or because you need the escape?"

"Both." Beth glanced around them to see if any coworkers were nearby. "I like my job because it's exactly what I need and has specific hours. But sometimes, it can get a little claustrophobic in the gift shop when it gets busy. I'd much rather work with kids, lead tours, or spend my time behind my computer screen." She pointed to the bag he'd brought. There were no obvious logos to hint at what might be inside. "All right, I took a big risk agreeing to let you bring lunch. Care to give a starving woman a hint?"

It looked like he might've considered making her wait before taking pity on her. "How about fried chicken, potato salad, cornbread, and lemonade?"

Her stomach growled immediately in response. They both laughed.

"I take it that's a good sign?"

Beth patted her stomach. "Absolutely."

"A woman who's not afraid to eat. You've scored a point in my book."

She wanted to ask what her overall score was but held her tongue. They walked to her usual spot, sat down to eat, and visited easily about general things that had happened to them over the course of the weekend.

She lifted a piece of chicken. "This is amazing. Where did you get it?"

"It's actually leftover from dinner last night. My dad fried it; he makes some of the best chicken around."

"No joke. Please tell him I said it was amazing."

"I will." Tyler smiled. "I bought the rest of the lunch at the store on the way here."

Beth laughed. "There's nothing wrong with that.

Thank you for bringing it." She wiped some grease from her hands onto a napkin. "I'm going to warn you up front that my friend, Monique, is outspoken. If you do come to the gift shop looking for me, don't be surprised if you get pounced on. She means well, but she's not the least bit shy."

"Unlike you." Tyler leaned back in his chair and studied her long enough to make Beth unsure of herself. When she reached for her ponytail, he pointed to it. "I've noticed you always keep your hair pulled back. Is there a reason?"

Beth shrugged. "It keeps it out of my way. I guess it's a habit." Why was he asking? She tried to discern whether he liked it up, preferred it down, or if it even mattered at all. See? This was why it drove her crazy to be focusing on what a guy thinks. It was much easier when she didn't care. Some of her internal conflict must've shown on her face, because Tyler raised a hand as though defending himself.

"I was just asking. I've only seen it down once when we came here to trick-or-treat. I think your hair looks beautiful no matter how you wear it. It's a very striking color." He seemed sincere.

She relaxed a little and even laughed at herself. It was ridiculous she was driving herself crazy like this. "Thank you. I guess I usually tie it back for work. I hadn't really thought about it until you asked." Maybe she should leave it down more often. She always got compliments on it when she did. Her hair was one of the things people had complimented her on ever since she was a little girl.

He nodded toward her paper plate. "Are you finished?"

"I am. It was great, thank you again."

"You're welcome." He looked at his watch. "I have time if you'd like to take a short walk before I need to head back."

"Sure, that sounds nice." They both stood, and Beth smiled at him. They cleaned everything up and then walked together toward the side of the zoo that overlooked the nearby lake.

"Meg and I both like this area of the zoo the best. Although for vastly different reasons."

Beth stepped over a small puddle in the middle of the sidewalk. "Oh?"

"She likes to feed and watch the fish. I like the tranquility of the water, and daydream about catching said fish."

She chuckled as they came to the walkway that led to the small pier. Without thinking about it, they both turned and walked that direction. Several kids had fish food their parents got for them out of the dispenser and were busy tossing the pellets over the side.

Beth and Tyler stopped to peer at the fish that were trying so hard to snatch up a pellet or two that they were practically leaping out of the water. Beth wrinkled her nose at the foot-long carp and their wide mouths grazing the surface of the water. "I have to admit I'm with you on that one. I'd rather eat one of these guys than watch them. It's the making of a horror movie." Thinking about trying to swim with hundreds of the scaly animals grazing her body made her shiver.

Tyler must have interpreted it as a sign of being cold. Wordlessly, he took the jacket he'd been carrying and draped it over her shoulders. Cold or not, it was incredibly sweet. His clean scent enveloped her. "Thank you."

"You're welcome." He gave her a smile that nearly had her heart melting into her shoes.

~

Tyler led the way to the end of the pier where they both leaned against the railing. Most of the fish and even a few turtles were down where the kids were throwing food. That left only the rogue critters swimming around. A large red-eared slider surfaced, the sun gleaming off his turtle shell. But it was the barely visible reflection of Beth's face in the water that held his attention.

Tyler finally turned his head to look at her. "Do you like to fish? Or just eat fish in general?"

"I haven't gone fishing in years. I used to go with my brother when we were young and always enjoyed it." She laughed. "There used to be an old tire swing by the pond. We'd go down and fish for a while, then we'd go swimming. I was on the tire swing that went out over the water when the rope snapped and sent me plunging. I was convinced he cut it on purpose, and it was two days before I finally believed him. He never let me forget I screamed like a little girl when it fell, either."

Tyler laughed but felt the all too familiar pang of loneliness. "It must've been nice to have so many siblings."

"Most of the time. I tended to be less…how should I put it? High maintenance than my older sisters. It seemed like they were always getting in trouble. Then Lance was in the police force for a while. I made it my place in the family to keep the peace and try to smooth things over between everyone else." She turned away from the water to face him and leaned with her elbows behind her on the railing.

"Does it work?" Tyler enjoyed the way the slight breeze was toying with the strands of hair by her cheek. His fingers itched to take her ponytail out and watch the long, blonde hair flow around her shoulders.

"I'd say about fifty percent of the time." Her eyes twinkled. "How about you? What was it like for you growing up?"

He shrugged. "I'm an only child, and it certainly had its highlights. I had my parents' nearly undivided attention and didn't have to share much. But it also got lonely, especially after my mom died. It wasn't the same for me or my dad after that."

"I'm sorry." Her red lips pulled down in a frown. "How old were you?"

"Twelve. She had a heart attack, and we were completely unprepared."

"I can imagine." Beth crossed her arms in front of her. "My dad had a stroke a couple of years ago. We had no idea, either. Thankfully, he made it, but he's had a lot of mobility issues since. It's been rough on him. I'm thankful every day that he's still here, though." She reached a hand out and gently touched Tyler's arm before pulling back again. "I'm sorry you lost your mom at such a young age."

"I appreciate it." He wanted to get their conversation back to a happier topic. "I guess that's life, right? Sometimes it's amazing, and sometimes it's a real kick in the teeth."

"Isn't that the truth?"

Beth's little laugh drew Tyler's attention to her mouth. He shifted his gaze to her eyes. They softened as she focused on his face. "I'm glad I let you talk me into lunch."

"I'm glad you did, too." Unable to stop himself any longer, he reached out and tucked a wayward strand of hair behind her ear. He wasn't sure which was softer: the hair or her skin. "Is there any chance I could see you next weekend? Maybe we could go fishing or something fun like that. If I pay for a couple of movie tickets, I'm pretty sure Dad will be happy to keep Meg for the day." Tyler watched her face closely, hoping she'd say yes.

Her mouth pulled to one side as she thought about it. "Wow, Thursday's Thanksgiving, isn't it? Is it just going to be you, Meg, and your dad?"

"Yeah. It's usually a pretty quiet day." He swallowed hard. Truthfully, the holidays were some of the hardest days of the year. Even though Meg now made them fun and full of laughter, they were the days Tyler remembered his mom the most.

"You should all come over for Thanksgiving."

Beth looked about as surprised by her invitation as Tyler was. "I wouldn't want to intrude."

"Trust me, you won't be. It won't be as overwhelming since not all of my family will be there. You won't be imposing, especially if you bring a side dish and a dessert."

The glitter of hope in her eyes sparked some inside him as well. "That's a wonderful offer. Let me talk to Dad and see what he thinks. Can I call you tonight or tomorrow and let you know?"

"Of course." She paused. "My family is pretty intense. They're going to insist there's something going on between us if I'm bringing you to the house. I'm hoping the fact that you're coming with Meg and your dad will help our case."

Suddenly, the thought of her family thinking they were together held more than a little appeal. He took a step closer and breathed in the scent of her hair wafting on the breeze. "If we come for Thanksgiving, does that mean a no to getting together and going fishing or something the next day?"

The corners of her mouth tugged upward. "Not necessarily."

Everything about her, from the way she was looking at him to how her mouth begged to be kissed, drew him closer. Tyler's lips were inches from hers when a young child ran across the pier in their direction, tripped, and landed on the wooden planks. His handful of fish food scattered at their feet.

His parents reached him in moments, but he was already crying earnestly.

Reluctantly, Tyler took a step back from Beth, their moment interrupted. "I guess I'd better escort you back to the gift shop. I should probably head out and let Dad take a lunch."

They turned and walked back to the main part of the zoo. Tyler resisted the need to reach for her hand as they strolled together toward the front of the zoo again. Once there, they turned toward each other.

Beth brushed some hair out of her face and smiled. "I had fun. Thanks for bringing lunch, and don't forget to tell your dad I said his chicken is fantastic."

"I won't. I had a lot of fun, too. I'll call you tonight about Thanksgiving." He nodded toward the building behind her. "Don't work too hard." He almost asked her to call him if she needed something, but she had sisters, a brother, and her parents nearby. It was highly unlikely she'd choose him to call in any kind of emergency.

"Same to you."

They waved at each other in that almost awkward way, and Tyler turned to leave. All the way back to the shop, he thought about the different ways he could convince his dad to go to the Davenport's place for Thanksgiving.

Chapter Nine

Beth chopped the potatoes she'd peeled and dropped the smaller pieces into a pot. They hit the water with a splunk, sending droplets onto the stovetop with a sizzle. "Surely this is enough. I'm pretty sure I've peeled enough potatoes to feed half of Kitner."

Mom looked into the pot and nodded. "That's good. People will trickle in anytime now, but I want to make sure we have everything ready for dinner." Mom always had been punctual on eating times. If she said they were eating Thanksgiving dinner at six, you'd better be there at five forty-five or you risked missing out.

Beth cleaned up the potato mess and released her hair from its low ponytail. She'd gathered it to keep hair out of the food, but intended to leave it down. Her family would laugh if they knew how long she'd agonized over such a silly decision this morning before coming over. Was she leaving it down for Tyler? No. Well, maybe. Did it even matter?

The doorbell rang, and she heard Dad get up from watching football to answer the door.

Moments later, Lexi came in with two large bags in her arms. "Hi everyone! Happy Thanksgiving." She set her things down on the counter and gave them both a hug.

"I'm glad you guys could make it today." Mom gave Lexi another squeeze. "Are you celebrating with your mom tomorrow?"

Lexi pulled a casserole dish out of one bag and slid it into the fridge. That alone was like playing a game of Tetris when it came to finding an available spot. "Yes. Tuck's working today and Serenity can't get in until tomorrow. We're going to have Thanksgiving a day late." She grinned and rubbed her midsection. "As if two dinners is a bad thing—it's worth the extra pounds." Her shoulder-length dark hair swished around her face as she turned and got two flats of rolls out of the other bag.

The doorbell rang again, and Mom perked up. "I'll bet that's Avalon, Duke, and Lorelei. I'd better go give that grandbaby a hug!" She brushed her hands off on the apron she was wearing and hurried out of the room.

Beth exchanged an amused look with Lexi. "It's nice to know where we stand, right?"

Lexi was still chuckling when Avalon breezed into the room, her arms full of covered dishes. "Hi ladies." She smiled brightly. "I brought the stuffing and the fruit salad. Where do we want them?"

They were still organizing when the doorbell rang again. Avalon and Lexi blinked at each other. "Isn't everyone here?" Avalon asked. "Marian's family wasn't coming, were they?"

"No, but they'll be here for Christmas." Lexi looked perplexed.

Beth cleared her throat. "I meant to tell you guys I invited some people to join us who didn't have anywhere to go for Thanksgiving. I didn't think anyone would mind." She left the others behind and hurried to the living room. She hated for Tyler and his father to face the rest of her family alone, especially the guys.

Dad had already opened the door and ushered their guests in. Lance immediately caught Beth's eyes from across the room and gave her a playful wink. She returned it with what she hoped was a look that inspired him to behave himself.

"Everyone, this is Bill, his son, Tyler." She smiled at Meg. "And that little princess is Tyler's daughter, Meg."

Meg waved briefly and then ran to Beth who crouched to accept the big hug. "I've been so excited for today. Do you like turkey? I could eat a hundred of them."

"I love turkey, too." Beth chuckled and stood again, briefly making eye contact with Tyler. His warm gaze as he watched them interact had her fighting to keep the heat from her face. She smoothed the bottom of her shirt, trying to act as normal as possible. "I see you met my dad, Peter. This is my mom, Vera." She pointed to Lance. "You met my brother, Lance. This guy here is Duke."

Duke shook hands with both of their guests. Lexi and Avalon came into the room then, and Beth continued the introductions. "Avalon is my sister and she's married to Duke. That little cutie in my mom's arms is their daughter, Lorelei. Then this is Lexi, the woman who took pity on my only brother and married him."

Lance walked across the room and put an arm around Lexi. "Isn't that the truth?" He kissed her on the cheek, and Lexi gave him a loving smile.

Bill gave a nod. "It's great to meet you all. We appreciate you letting us crash for Thanksgiving dinner."

"You're more than welcome," Mom said as she patted Lorelei's back. "Come on in and make yourself at home. Beth, take that from them, will you?"

Beth was happy to see Tyler's father accept her dad's invitation to join him in watching the football game. She noticed the items in Tyler's hand for the first time. "I'm sorry! Of course, let me get those for you."

He handed a pie tin to her but kept the others. "If you'll show me where you want to put these, I'll follow you."

"Sure." Beth did her best to act normally while her heart was doing cartwheels in her chest. She'd invited a guy home for Thanksgiving dinner. Granted, it was a great thing to give them some place to celebrate—a good deed, even. But when it was all said and done, she'd invited a guy home.

She tried not to compare this—whatever this was—with her previous relationship. She wanted to enjoy today, and refused to give any of that up.

As they left the living room, she noticed Mom had put Lorelai on the floor and was introducing her to Meg.

Beth and Tyler entered the kitchen. Beth lifted the pie pan in her hands. "What do we have here?"

"Pecan pie. It doesn't need to be refrigerated."

"Perfect." She found a space for it on the dessert counter.

Tyler put the large pan he held on the stove top. "This is hominy casserole, and it'll stay warm enough up here until it's time to eat."

"Hominy casserole? I've never heard of that." She looked at the container curiously.

"It was my mom's recipe. She made it every Christmas and Thanksgiving, and Dad's carried on the tradition since. We figured it wasn't likely to be a repeat of whatever everyone else brought." He chuckled. He tipped his head toward the living room. "Your family seems really nice."

"They're awesome, and I'm glad you think so. I hope you still do after you've been questioned thoroughly after dinner." Yeah, and she was only partially kidding. There was no way he was going to get through the evening without going through some kind of inquisition. "They'll want to know if there's anything between us."

"Is there?" Tyler took a step toward her.

Beth swallowed hard. "Is there what?"

He gave her a look that suggested she knew exactly what he was referring to. "I want to make sure we're on the same page when they ask."

Completely thrown off track, Beth stammered, "I...I..." The kitchen door opened letting Mom, Avalon, and Lexi inside. Great. Hopefully her face wasn't as bright red as she felt like it was. She swung to the stove and stirred the gravy. The burner wasn't on yet, but it made her look like she was doing something.

"I figured we should finish up some details for dinner. We'll be eating in twenty minutes." Mom gave Tyler a kind smile. "Thank you and your father for contributing to the meal. We're glad you could join us. Beth hasn't brought a friend to dinner in a long time."

There was a slight emphasis on the word "friend" that Beth chose to ignore.

"Well, I'm glad to be here. I'm happy to help if there's anything I can do."

Beth looked over her shoulder in time to see his offer earned a smile from Mom. "I appreciate that, but why don't you go ahead and hang out with the guys. We've got this."

"If you're sure." Tyler tossed Beth a subtle wink and left the room.

"Where'd you meet him?" Lexi asked as she started to pull containers of food out of the fridge. "He seems to like you."

"He sure does." Avalon leaned against the counter. "So why haven't I heard about this hunky guy before?"

Beth pointed to him. "This is why." She shook her head but couldn't quite keep the amusement off her face. She lowered her voice. "It's not a big deal. I'm still getting to know him. He and his family didn't have anywhere to go for Thanksgiving, and I hated to think of them alone for the holiday. I thought I'd invite them to join us."

Avalon grinned, a knowing look in her eyes. "And I'm sure it's a hardship having him here, too."

Mom clapped her hands together, all business. "All right, girls. Let's get this meal on the table!"

~

Tyler hadn't laughed that much in a long time. To say Beth's family was a blast was an understatement. He didn't think they teased each other any more than he and Dad did, but there were many more of them. To think not all the siblings were there today. He could only imagine how much more wonderfully chaotic it could get.

Little Lorelai seemed to love all the attention she got from her family. Duke said the baby was only sixteen months old, but she ran all over the place like a champ. When she did fall, she got right back up again as if she couldn't be bothered by wasting time otherwise. While the cute little girl bounced from family member to family member, it was clear one of her favorite places to be was Beth's arms.

At the moment, Beth was sitting in the rocking chair with both Meg and Lorelai on her lap. Beth was singing the words to a book she held. The din in the living room made it impossible for Tyler to catch all the words. There was no doubt, though, that she had both girls' interest. The toddler watched her aunt, fingers in her mouth, with adoration. And Meg? She was soaking in the attention.

Tyler never thought seeing an image like that would stir up such a mix of emotions. On one hand, it nearly killed him that Meg had never experienced that kind of love from her mother or any other woman in her life. He knew he and Dad were doing a good job with Meg, but there was something about a mother's love that they couldn't replace.

On the other hand, watching Beth like this brought images to his mind he shouldn't be entertaining. Images of Beth holding a little girl with her blue eyes and his dark hair in one arm, while she cuddled Meg with the other.

Beth caught him watching her. She raised her hand in a shy half-wave and smiled self-consciously.

Everything about her, from the way she

interacted with the kids to how she treated others around her, spoke of how special she was. Tyler decided then that he wanted to keep her in his life. He wasn't sure what that meant, but he looked forward to figuring it out.

A thunderous cheer reminded Tyler that he was supposed to be watching the football game. It was fun to see Dad having such a great Thanksgiving. He and Peter seemed to hit it off and had talked about everything from what they did for work to football to the state of the world.

It'd been nearly two hours since they ate dinner, yet it'd flown by. Tyler added today to his list of some of his favorite holiday memories. He was so lost in thought, he hardly noticed anything until a shadow fell on him. He found Beth watching him, and a quick glance around the room revealed Meg and Lorelai were playing on the floor.

Beth's brows drew together. "Everything okay?"

"Everything is fine." He nodded toward the chair where she'd been reading to the girls earlier. "You've got a way with kids. I think your niece is totally taken with you, and Meg's not far behind."

"The feeling's mutual." Beth smiled fondly. "I think Lorelai is loving all of this attention. My sister, Marian, and her husband have four kids, and then Gwen has a new baby. When all the cousins are here, attention's a little more divided." She leaned against the arm of the couch where Tyler was sitting. "But I get to see Lorelai a lot since we all live in Kitner."

The ends of her hair tickled his arm. The fact that her hair flowed down her back was one of the first things he'd noticed when he saw her today. She'd probably worn it down for the holiday, but there was a little part of him that hoped she'd done it for him, too. Tyler resisted the urge to reach for her hand. "I'm glad a lot of your family is close by. That's a real blessing."

"It is. Especially when everyone gets along most of the time."

The combination of her proximity with that sweet laughter was like torture. He stifled a groan. She wasn't making it easy for him to keep his hands to himself, but with all her family around, he wasn't about to put her in a difficult position with any public displays of affection. Especially when he wasn't completely sure if they would be welcomed.

Vera came into the room from the kitchen and raised her voice to be heard over the game. "Who's ready for some dessert?"

Affirmative mutters echoed around the room in combination with sympathetic pats to full stomachs. Beth stood away from the couch. "It doesn't matter how much I eat at dinner, there's always room for dessert."

"I couldn't agree with you more." Tyler followed suit and stretched his back a little. "I'm going to need to run a mile or two to work some of these calories off."

"You run? I didn't know that."

"I don't, but I probably should, though."

Beth laughed at that. Tyler decided that he'd make it his mission to find ways to get her to laugh every day he was around her.

Almost everyone, including Meg, headed toward the kitchen, leaving Tyler, Beth, and Lance alone in the living room. Lance approached them with a serious look on his face.

He focused his attention on Tyler. "So, are you

two officially seeing each other?"

Beth warned Tyler, but he hadn't expected such a direct question. He had no idea what he was supposed to say to that. Thankfully, Beth jumped right in with a response.

"We haven't had a chance to..." She stopped and hedged a look at Tyler. "Maybe."

Lance gave Tyler a firm look. "Remember to treat my little sister here with the kind of respect you'll want someone to show your daughter one day, and we'll be fine." He smiled then and held his hand out. "Real glad you could come over for dinner today."

Tyler suppressed a whoosh of air as he exhaled in relief and gratefully shook Lance's hand. "I appreciate the warm welcome, and I'll remember what you said."

He looked at Beth to find her cheeks flushed but a pleased look on her face.

Lexi peeked around the corner from the kitchen and locked eyes with Lance. It was clear she knew what they'd been talking about. She gave him a look that was somewhere between humor and a warning. "There you are. Hey, Beth, I almost forgot." She entered the room, her phone in her hand. She swiped the screen. "The hospital's asking for volunteers for this year's Operation: Joy. Did you want to sign up again? It's the third Saturday of December."

"Of course, I'll put in for the vacation. I told my boss that was coming up."

"Awesome!" Lexi grinned as she typed something into her phone. "Do you have a preference on station?"

"I'll deliver plates of cookies like last year."

Tyler was feeling lost as his attention went back

and forth between the women. "What's this for?"

Lance put an arm around Lexi. "My sweet wife here volunteers in the NICU over at the hospital. She's on the committee as well. Every year, the hospital serves Christmas dinner for everyone who can get to the cafeteria. For those who can't, a meal or dessert is taken to their hospital rooms. Santa Claus makes an appearance for the kids, and gifts are donated for all the patients. It's a big thing."

It was clear how proud Lance was of his wife and what she was doing for the community.

"Wow, that's incredible. I had no idea."

Lexi's grin lit up her face. "And my sister-in-law here has helped the last three years. We couldn't do it without her." A mischievous look twinkled in her eyes. "You know, we can always use more volunteers. I don't suppose you'd be interested in helping us out this year."

Well, that was the last thing Tyler expected. He looked to Lance who only smothered a smile and gave a small shrug.

"What time is it?"

"Volunteers usually stay from five until seven. Others stay a lot longer, but if you could commit to the two-hour block, that'd be great."

Now Lexi exuded so much hope there was no way Tyler could say no. Add in the fact that it'd mean spending some time with Beth, and he was ready to agree. "I think I could make that work. Can you go ahead and add me to the roster? I'll need to make sure Dad's okay with watching Meg that night, but I don't think it'll be a problem."

"Sure thing." Lexi tapped something into her phone. She looked up again. "You want to deliver cookies too?" She gave Beth a not-so-subtle smile.

"Sounds good." He liked the way his answer made Beth's cheeks turn an even darker pink.

Lance planted a kiss on Lexi's cheek. "Alright, we'd better get into the kitchen before dessert's gone and we're left with crumbs."

Tyler caught Beth's eye and made a motion toward the kitchen. "Ladies first."

An hour later, after everyone had filled up with desserts, people started to get ready to leave. Vera insisted on fixing a plate of leftovers for Tyler's family, something which Tyler looked forward to eating tomorrow.

After wishing everyone a happy Thanksgiving, Tyler, Dad, and Meg headed back outside. Beth said she'd walk them out and followed.

"I'm glad you could join us. I hope my family behaved themselves."

Dad chuckled. "Everyone was wonderful, Beth, thank you for inviting us. This was one of the most enjoyable Thanksgivings we've had in years." He surprised her with a hug.

Meg gave Beth a gigantic embrace. "I had a ton of fun. I hope we can come back again tomorrow." It was clear from her expression she meant what she said. They all chuckled at her.

Dad reached for Meg's hand. "Come on, girl, let's go get in the car and give these two a few minutes to chat."

For the first time in hours, Tyler found himself alone with Beth. He rubbed the back of his neck. "Well, that was anything but subtle."

Beth tilted her head toward her parents' house and the pair of faces barely discernable as they watched through the window. "Yeah, I know what you mean." She grinned. "It was fun having you all here, and the hominy casserole was good. I'd never had it before, but I'll have to add it as a must-have for next year."

Tyler started to turn toward his car but hesitated. "I hope I didn't overstep my bounds agreeing to volunteer at the hospital. If you'd rather I call Lexi and tell her I can't make it, please let me know."

Beth had started shaking her head before he'd finished talking. "I think it'll be fun to work together. I'm going to warn you, though, it's two hours of going to almost every nook and cranny of that hospital. It's a workout."

"I'm looking forward to it." He glanced at the car and his waiting family. "I'd still like to see you this weekend. How would you like to go fishing and have a picnic on Sunday after church?" Beth's eyes widened at the offer. "Or we can see a movie, if you'd rather stay indoors. You name the activity."

She glanced at the house again before putting her hands in her back pockets and putting her weight on one foot and then the other. "I think fishing and a picnic sounds like fun."

"Great. I'll text you tonight and figure out the time. Or maybe I'll call you instead." If it weren't for the fact that his dad was waiting right behind him and who knows how many people were watching from the house, Tyler would've kissed Beth. Instead, he smiled again. "I didn't get the chance to say it earlier. You look beautiful today." He turned toward the car. "I guess we'd better get home. I think I'm going to need a nap to sleep off this turkey coma. Goodbye, Beth, I'll talk to you soon."

"Bye, Tyler."

He noticed that she stayed on the curb and watched them until they'd driven out of sight.

Chapter Ten

I have to ask." Tyler opened the small cooler and fished out a container of worms. "Are you the type of woman who says she's been fishing, and then wants someone else to put a worm on your hook? Or do you bait your own?"

His question caused Beth to smile. She stuck a hand out, palm up. "I can bait my own hook. Worms don't scare me." Well, they didn't now, anyway. She chuckled. "Though that wasn't always the case. One time, when I was seven or so, Lance poured a whole container of them down my shirt. I'd have beaten him up if he weren't so much bigger than me." Lance had put a hand on her head, and that's all it took to keep her swinging arms at bay. They both laughed about it now.

Tyler seemed quite amused. "Most of the girls I knew in school would've jumped up and down screaming if someone had dumped worms down their shirts."

"When you're the youngest of five, you just get

even." Beth laughed.

"Your family was great at Thanksgiving. Dad and I both had fun, and Meg couldn't stop talking about you and Lorelai."

"That's sweet." Beth finished baiting her hook and wiped her hand off on the rag he provided. "I know Lorelai had a lot of fun with her, too."

They sat side by side in silence as they cast their lines and waited for a bite. Beth didn't mind the quiet. There was little activity at the lake now that it was near the end of November. The first freeze was likely going to happen soon. She looked up at the leaves still clinging to the branches of the trees. Most falls, the leaves hung on until that first freeze, and then dropped to the ground a shade of dark brown or black. One of these days, she wanted to go somewhere where she could see a true fall full of yellows, reds, and browns.

"Have you always lived in Kitner?" she asked Tyler.

"All my life. You?"

She nodded. "Me, too. Isn't it weird we've never met before? Funny to think we've lived in the same town all this time." She wished she'd met him before Carl. The thought made her a little sad. Beth didn't realize her emotions were showing on her face until Tyler bumped her shoulder gently with his.

"Penny for your thoughts. What's got you down? If you're worried about the worm..." One corner of his mouth quirked up in amusement.

Beth laughed. "No, I'm not worried about the worm. I was thinking about the curve balls life throws at us." She hesitated, uncertain how much to say. "I wonder what it would've been like if I'd met you a couple of years ago. Before..."

"Before everything with your ex?" She nodded. "I wonder the same thing sometimes. I don't regret everything with Reece because if it weren't for that, I wouldn't have Meg. She's my whole world. But knowing you now makes me wish I'd met you years ago."

"Really?" She held her breath, her pulse racing.

"Yes, really." He'd turned partially to see her better, his dark eyes holding her gaze. He held his fishing pole with the left hand, and let his right arm rest against one knee. He reached a single finger out to brush her arm.

Even with the long-sleeved shirt, she could feel his finger as though it were searing through the fabric and touching her skin. In that moment, all she wanted him to do was kiss her. It wasn't rational, but she didn't care. She wanted to feel his lips against hers and find out what it'd be like to be held by him.

Her fishing pole jerked, and she nearly dropped it in surprise. "Oh!" Whatever fish had taken a bite, it was pulling hard. Beth scrambled to her feet and reeled it in faster. Tyler stood with her. She got the fish close enough to shore they could see the pale form beneath the surface of the water. The line became slack and she reeled it in the rest of the way.

Tyler pointed to the barren hook. "It was hungry. I hate to say it, but your worm is a goner."

Beth shrugged. "Put the poor thing out of its misery."

He handed his fishing pole to her. "Take mine, and I'll bait yours again for you."

"Thanks."

Over the next hour, they both got several more bites but didn't manage to catch anything. They finally gave up and decided to eat lunch. After cleaning up, they sat on the blanket Beth brought.

They'd both agreed to avoid chicken or turkey after Thanksgiving. Instead, he'd picked up ham sub sandwiches, chips, and sweet iced tea. Beth's stomach rumbled as she took her first bite. "You know what? I love turkey, I do. But between Thanksgiving and Christmas, I'm always happy to eat anything that isn't poultry."

He laughed. "I agree. Do you all get together like that for Christmas, too?"

"Normally. This year, though, I think we're doing a mega Christmas celebration." When he looked at her quizzically, she explained. "We know Lexi's family well. Instead of Lance and Lexi having to choose where to celebrate this year, we thought the two families would have Christmas together. All four of my siblings will be there, and Lexi and her two. It's going to be a madhouse, but it'll be fun."

"That would be amazing. Like the kind of Christmases I imagined as a child."

His voice sounded wistful, and Beth had to keep herself from reaching out to touch him.

He shook his head as if he were trying to release a memory. "And then my Meg came along. She keeps things interesting, especially at Christmas. You should see the wish list she put together: Santa's going to be hard-pressed to narrow down his choices this year."

Beth pictured the spirited little girl and could imagine her excitement on Christmas morning. She wished she could see it. In fact, she wished she could spend Christmas with Tyler and Meg. She almost invited him to join them but thought better of it. But they were likely going to the Chandler house, and she couldn't invite someone without asking them first.

"I'm glad you suggested this. Even if we aren't catching anything, it's great to be outside for a while. Who knows how much longer this mild weather's going to last?"

Tyler wadded up the wrapper from his sandwich and put it back in the large cooler he'd brought. After looking around inside for a moment, he withdrew a small bag. "For dessert, I have chocolate chip cookies." He paused, giving her a serious look. "Please tell me you like chocolate chip cookies."

Beth laughed. "Who doesn't?" She gladly accepted the treat and took a bite. "Mmmm this is good, thank you."

He polished off his cookie in several bites and looked up at the tree blocking the sun above them. "This is my favorite time of year."

"Mine, too. Well, this and spring." Beth finished her cookie and brushed her hands off on her pants. "I don't mind winter going into it, but by the time February comes around, I'm more than ready for warmer weather and flowers."

"And what is your favorite flower?"

"I like daisies. They always make me happy."

"I'll remember that." He smiled at her. "I've enjoyed seeing you over the last few days. I wish we didn't have to go back to a normal schedule tomorrow."

"I wish we didn't, either." She caught a stray strand of hair that'd come loose from her French braid and wound it around her finger.

He shifted closer to her, his attention on her face. "You are beautiful, Beth. I thought that the moment I saw you, even with the crazy mess of losing Meg that day."

Beth swallowed hard, her face warm under his gaze. What was she supposed to say? That he was handsome? That she enjoyed spending time with him? That he constantly occupied her thoughts?

He must have understood her silence because he reached for her hand and held it in his. "I'd like to start seeing you. Officially." He looked flustered then, and Beth thought it was adorable.

"I'd like that, too."

"Oh, yeah?"

"Yes." She smiled at him.

"Good. I thought I'd drop by the zoo and have lunch with you on Wednesday. I'd come tomorrow, but we've got an unusually full schedule after the long weekend."

"Wednesday sounds good." Beth was pretty sure her grin was now permanently etched into her face.

Tyler's happy expression shifted. Curiosity and determination mixed in the depth of his dark eyes. "There's something I've wanted to do since we took a walk at the zoo."

"Oh? What's that?"

He gently cupped her right cheek with his hand before closing the gap between them. The moment his lips touched hers, Beth thought she was going to melt right into the ground. Her hand went to his neck, her fingertips grazing his short hair.

Tyler put an arm around her waist and deepened the kiss. When he pulled back again, Beth's head swam. She resisted the urge to put her fingers to her lips.

"It's official." His voice sounded husky.

"What's that?"

"This is the best fishing trip I've ever been on."

That makes two of us.

~

"Daddy? Don't forget to ask her today." Meg pulled her shoes on and grabbed her backpack off the nearby chair. "Tell her it's going to be at the pizza place and there'll be games. Oh! And don't forget to tell her it's the new place, not that yucky old one." She wrinkled her nose.

Tyler might have laughed at her antics and cute expression if this weren't the fifth time she'd brought up the subject since she woke this morning. "Baby, what did I say?"

Meg paused and then frowned a little. "That you would ask her, and if she can come, you'll make sure she knows where we're having my party. Sorry. I'm just *so* excited. I want Beth to come more than anyone else!"

He did, too. Asking her to join them for his daughter's seventh birthday was a big step. Or at least, it could seem like one. If he told Beth that Meg was inviting her to come, that was one thing. If he told her that *he* hoped she'd come, it was something else entirely. In that case, it was him inviting her into a more intimate part of his life. Including her in his family.

Or was he completely overthinking the whole thing? Probably. Not that it mattered because he was going to ask her regardless. There was no point in worrying about how it would appear.

Tyler gave Meg a little nudge. "Take your glass to the sink, and let's get you to school."

Meg gulped the last of her orange juice, did as she was told, and still beat him to the front door.

Dad had been at the shop for an hour. Tyler would drop Meg off at school, work for a while, and then meet Beth at the zoo for lunch.

Just thinking about it gave him more energy than he usually had this early in the morning.

They made it to school right on time. He then rushed to the shop where Dad was waiting.

"Sorry, Dad. It was hard getting Meg out of the house this morning." Tyler rolled his sleeves up and got to work. "All she'd talk about was her birthday and making sure Beth was going to be there."

"She sure likes that gal, doesn't she?" Dad stopped what he was doing and looked at Tyler. "I've never seen her do that before."

"Me, either. Last year, it was all about making sure her whole class was invited. This year, it's all about Beth."

"Are you second-guessing your decision to invite her?" Dad's expression was frustratingly neutral.

"Should I be? What if Meg gets too attached and something happens?"

Dad frowned. "Are you worried about Meg or yourself?"

Good question. "Maybe both. I can handle it, but I'm not sure I could stand to watch another woman walk away from my little girl."

Dad gave a nod, satisfied with Tyler's answer. "Life is about risks: Weighing your choices and determining whether the risk is worth taking." He went back to work, leaving Tyler to mull over his words.

Risks. Wasn't that the truth? He didn't like the idea of Meg being hurt, but no woman had intrigued him like Beth. He was drawn to her in a way he couldn't explain. Maybe it was a risk to let her into their lives, yet the thought of not exploring the possibilities of a relationship with her seemed like a risk as well.

There was nothing he could do about it now. He focused on his work and made it through the morning relatively quickly. After promising he'd bring lunch back for Dad, he swung by his favorite burger place and headed for the zoo.

He got there early enough to meet Beth at the gift shop. Her bright smile, in combination with the fact that she'd left her hair down to flow around her shoulders, swept away all the doubts swirling in the back of his mind since this morning. "Hey, beautiful." He gave her a brief kiss on the cheek, aware that Monique was watching them with a grin. Tyler offered Beth an arm. "Ready to go?"

"Very." She turned and waved to Monique. "I'll be back in a bit."

"Enjoy!"

Tyler whisked Beth out of the gift shop and into the cool air outside. He glanced down at her attire. "Do you need a jacket?"

She tugged on the long sleeves of her purple zoo shirt and shook her head. "I'm good. It's been horribly stuffy inside today. Even if I get cold, it'll be a welcome change."

He noticed she didn't have the canvas bag or laptop with her. "No computer today?"

She shook her head. "I didn't figure I'd be writing while we had lunch. I left it at home."

He'd wondered what she was using the laptop for, and this seemed like a good opening to ask. "What do you use it for?" He hadn't expected his question to bring a look of panic and something else he couldn't quite identify.

"I write books."

Her voice was so quiet, he almost didn't hear her. "Books? Really?" That completely intrigued him. "What kind of books? Are you published?"

"I write for kids." She peeked at him. "I'm independently publishing my first title. I'm still trying to decide on a release date."

Tyler stopped, and it took a moment before Beth did as well. "Are you kidding? That's amazing." His mind raced as he tried to imagine what kind of children's book she might have written. "I had no idea."

"It's something I've always wanted to do. I've written for years, but I'm only now approaching it seriously." She seemed pleased he was taking an interest in her books.

"I'd like to read it sometime."

Pink traveled up Beth's neck and into her face. "Maybe Meg could test read an early copy for me."

That Beth was willing to share what she'd written meant a lot to him. "I'm sure she'd love that."

They continued walking. "I brought burgers and fries." He held up the bag. "I didn't think about it until today, but I'm surprised I haven't been reprimanded for bringing food into the zoo." He reached for her hand and held it as they walked.

"Normally you would be, but Monique knows why you're here, and we're eating in one of the places we employees have been told we could eat whatever we bring for lunch. There isn't a lot of choice at the snack bar here otherwise." She craned her neck to see the logo on the bag he carried. "Though I imagine most people here are going to be jealous."

Tyler chuckled. "A lot of guys might be jealous

of me for another reason." He lifted her hand to his lips and brushed them against her knuckles.

Beth ducked her chin, her hair falling forward, but not before he caught the smile on her face.

Chapter Eleven

Beth savored the spoonful of tomato soup and studied Avalon across the table. "Is it weird that I'm going to his kid's birthday party?"

Avalon's lips quirked up in amusement. "Unless you're planning on jumping into the ball pit or something, it's not weird."

Tyler had made it clear she wasn't obligated to go to Meg's birthday party a week from Saturday unless she wanted to, but there was no missing the sparkle in his eyes when she'd agreed. It'd only been in the twenty-four hours since that she started to second-guess her decision.

Lorelai tore her grilled cheese sandwich to bits, smearing melted cheese on the tray of her high chair, before finally settling down to eat the ragged pieces. "Ummmm! Good!"

"I couldn't agree more." Beth took an exaggerated bite of her own sandwich much to the amusement of her niece. Sometimes, the simplicity of a sandwich and a bowl of soup made the best meal.

Especially with the cooler weather that rolled in this morning and the first freeze of the season predicted for tonight. Beth wasn't looking forward to leading tours once the cold weather truly arrived. She dipped one corner of her sandwich in the soup and took another bite. "This hits the spot. You make the best tomato soup."

Avalon laughed. "It's from a can."

"I know, but you always made it better than anyone else. I'm serious, I can taste the difference."

"Maybe it's my secret ingredient," Avalon said cryptically.

"I'm not going to ask."

They ate in silence for a few moments before Avalon spoke again. "Why are you worried? Is there something about Tyler that you're nervous about?"

Beth thought about that and shook her head. "Not really. It's just... I had no idea about Carl, either. What if I have no real woman's intuition, or even common sense? What if I'm one of those women who always attracts the wrong type of guy?"

Avalon set her spoon in her bowl and frowned. "You don't truly believe that, do you? Carl was an anomaly. He had us all fooled." When Beth didn't look convinced, she continued. "You do have common sense, you left him as soon as he—"

After a quick glance at Lorelai, Beth held up a hand to stop her sister. She hated talking about Carl and everything that happened. "Well, it wasn't soon enough." Her next spoonful of soup was flavorless. "Tyler knows I had an ex and it wasn't pretty, but do I have to tell him details? I do, don't I?"

"You probably should at some point, but things are still new. I don't think you have to yet if you're not comfortable with it." Avalon reached across the table and patted her sister's hand. "Tyler isn't Carl."

That was true, and Beth would do well to remember that, but that was only part of her concern. She blamed Carl for the majority of what happened. Even still, she felt like she should've known what he was really like, and that's what she'd struggled with the most. If she didn't have the ability to see what someone was like before, had she changed enough in the last six months to trust herself? What if Carl weren't an anomaly, and it was a case of her being a bad judge of character?

Her thoughts must've shown on her face because, when she lifted her gaze to Avalon, her sister was looking at her with a sad expression. "I hate he still has such an effect on you. He's halfway across the country right now, if he knows what's good for him, but it's like he's still whispering in your ear."

Beth lost her grip on the spoon, and it splashed into her bowl. "I don't think that's true." Even she was surprised by how defensive she sounded. Lorelai paused in her eating to stare at her, mouth open. Beth forced herself to smile at her niece and brought her voice to a more normal tone.

The look of pity on Avalon's face made Beth's stomach roll. "All you've ever wanted was to become an author and to have a family. I'm glad you're finally pursuing one of those. I hate to see you give up the other because of a jerk who shouldn't be given the time of day. He's gone, Beth, but you're still letting him control you."

Beth wanted to object, even yell at Avalon and tell her she had no idea what she was talking about. Woodenly, she picked up her spoon and took another bite, trying desperately to school her features.

Avalon was right, though, as much as it pained Beth to admit it. She'd be lying if she said she didn't want a family of her own one day. Thinking about Tyler and Meg caused her heart to ache with the truth.

Tyler seemed great—almost too good to be true. What if he was, and she was being duped yet again? What if she finally let go of everything Carl did and allowed herself to hope again, only to have her heart broken? It was like waiting for the other shoe to drop.

She wondered how long she'd been staring at her tomato soup. When she glanced up, she found Avalon watching her, clearly concerned. "I'm trying."

"I know you are, Bethie. I'm praying for you. Everyone is."

That was good, she could certainly use all the help she could get. Beth sighed, no longer hungry. *God, am I ever going to stop second guessing myself? Please give me wisdom to know what to do when it comes to Tyler. With my life.*

After lunch with Avalon, Beth stopped by the store for a few things and headed home again. Beth stepped inside her place when her phone rang, making her jump. Tyler's name and number flashed on the screen as she answered.

"Hey."

"Hey yourself. Did you have a nice lunch with your sister?"

"We had a good visit." That was almost a lie, but Beth wasn't about to tell him their conversation or reveal the turmoil of emotions she was dealing with right now.

"That's great. Hey, Meg wanted to talk to you for a moment. Is that okay?"

Tyler's voice sounded carefree and happy. Beth envied him in that moment and said it would be great to talk to Meg on the phone.

Moments later, the little girl came on the line, her high-pitched voice even higher over the phone. "Hi Beth! Daddy says you're coming to my birthday party. I wanted you to know that I can't wait. Do you like middles or edges?"

Beth tried to figure out what she was referring to when she could hear Tyler talking the background.

Meg corrected herself. "Do you like pieces of cake from the middle, or from the edge with extra frosting?"

Beth smiled. "From the edge of course. Who doesn't love extra frosting?"

"That's the same as me! Okay, I'll make sure you get an edge piece on my birthday. And guess what? Daddy and Grandpa might take me to the zoo on Saturday. Isn't that awesome?"

"That's great, Meg. I'll be working that day, so I'm sure I'll see you."

"Alright. I'm going to hand you back to Daddy now. Bye!"

The girl's enthusiasm and never-ending energy had Beth almost tired listening to it. Tyler came back on the line. The sound of his deep chuckle rolled through Beth, doing more to soothe her than anything else had all day. She sank to the couch and tucked her legs beneath her. "I take it she's a little excited for her birthday."

"Oh, she's in the living room drawing invitations as we speak." There was no missing the affection in his voice. "It means a lot to her for you to come. Thank you for that."

"You're welcome. It'll be fun. Meg mentioned you might be coming to the zoo this weekend."

"I figured I should put that family pass to good use." His flirting tone was obvious even over the phone. "There might be a certain someone I'm hoping to see while we're there. You think that can be arranged?"

Beth couldn't stop her smile if she tried. "I'm sure I can figure something out."

How was it possible to feel so at ease when she spoke with him, yet second guess everything the moment they were apart?

~

Tyler hung an especially breakable ornament on a branch toward the top of the Christmas tree. The delicate glass angel held a trumpet to its lips, ready to announce the birth of Jesus Christ.

"That was always one of your mom's favorite ornaments."

Tyler hadn't heard Dad walk up behind him. He cleared his throat and nodded. "I remember. I think the whole tree would've been decorated with angels if she'd had her way."

"Nah." Dad went to one of the ornament boxes on the couch and withdrew a Santa made from a handprint. He gave it to Tyler. "She'd take these homemade ornaments any day."

Tyler marveled at the way the tiny Santa fit in his palm. It was hard to believe his hand was ever that small. He looked to Meg who was carefully arranging her small collection of sparkly ornaments at eye level. He was probably about her age when Mom helped him make the Santa.

The recollection brought fond memories and a wave of sadness in equal portions. He ought to take the time to make something like this with Meg. It's not like he didn't want to or didn't have the time; Tyler just never thought to do it. Crafts like these were something moms thought of. He put a lid on that thought before his mind wandered any further and brought his focus back to the cheery event at hand.

"What do you think, Daddy?" Meg stood back and motioned to the tree. "Isn't it pretty? I put the Tinkerbell next to my cupcake from last year in case she gets hungry. And Wonder Woman promised she'd protect them in case the Nutcracker decides to break into their clubhouse."

Tyler chuckled at the interesting conglomerate of ornaments she'd managed to collect. He bought her a new one each year. Keeping those traditions he'd experienced as a child were one of the ways they kept Mom's memory alive.

"It looks great, baby. Sounds like they've got everything figured out."

"They sure do." Meg lifted her Wonder Woman ornament, her choice this year. "I wish I could show her to Beth. I wonder if she'd want to play with me? Can we have her over to the house and show her our Christmas tree?"

"I don't know about that, but maybe you can tell her about it on Saturday."

That seemed to please Meg, and she went back to playing with her ornaments.

Tyler turned and met Dad's amused expression with a frown. "Don't start."

Dad only chuckled. "I'm not sure which of you

talks about Beth more."

"Yeah, whatever." He couldn't keep his laughter at bay. "Come on, let's get the rest of these on the tree."

~

Tyler held one of Meg's hands while Dad held the other. If they didn't, Tyler had no doubt she'd be running ahead in her hurry to find Beth at the zoo. Meg had even convinced him to take a picture of her Wonder Woman ornament to show Beth.

Truthfully, he couldn't wait to see Beth, either. They approached the gift shop, and Tyler opened the door, holding it wide so Dad and Meg could go inside. He immediately spotted Beth behind the counter helping a customer. "Let's browse for a few minutes while we wait for Beth to finish. That way we can say hi before we go look around the zoo."

He didn't have to tell Meg twice. She grabbed her grandpa's hand and pulled him toward the stuffed animals.

Tyler made notes about what caught Meg's attention, storing the information away for a possible Christmas gift.

The customer Beth was helping raised his voice, making it impossible for Tyler to not overhear.

"I thought I was supposed to get twenty percent off. I wouldn't have bought a membership otherwise." He slapped his large hand on the counter causing Beth to jump.

Beth's eyes widened a little, but she nodded and maintained an understanding smile. "I'm sorry for the confusion, but the twenty percent off is only on the day you purchase your membership. After that, it's ten percent off for the rest of the year." She observed the large number of small items on the counter. "Would you like me to cancel your transaction?"

The man picked something up and turned it over to look at the price. "Everything's way too expensive. Cancel it all." He brought it down quickly and slapped it onto the counter only inches from Beth.

She ducked her head and jumped away from the man as though he'd been about to strike her. The customer seemed surprised while Beth's face transformed from fear to shock and finally mortification. "I'll handle it. Again, I apologize for the confusion."

"Right." He tossed her an uncertain look and left.

Beth put her hands on the counter and leaned against it. Monique walked over and asked if she was okay. At that moment, Beth must have registered that Tyler was watching the exchange. She shook her head, said something as she jogged around the counter, and left through the back door.

Tyler looked for Dad and found him watching the whole thing as well. "I've got Meg, go ahead."

That was all he needed. Worried he wasn't going to get out fast enough to find her, he rushed after Beth. It only took a moment to spot her sitting on some bricks around the far side of the building. She had her knees pulled up to her chest, and her back to him.

As he approached her, he wondered what'd happened in the past to cause her to react that strongly to what the guy had done. Every other time he'd watched her work, she seemed cool as a cucumber. Beth must have heard his footsteps because she sat up straight and ran her hands over her face. He barely caught a muffled sniff as he sat down on the bricks beside her. "You okay?"

"Yeah. I'm fine, I just needed a minute." She wouldn't look directly at him, and her voice cracked, sounding anything but fine. She cleared her throat. "You should go back to your dad and Meg, I'm sure they're waiting for you."

"I'm not leaving until I'm convinced you're okay." He kept hoping she'd tell him the reason for her reaction, but she still said nothing. He reached a hand out and rested it on her shoulder. "What happened, Beth?"

She jumped to her feet. "My customer got confused about the discount, and I didn't do a good job explaining it. It was a miscommunication."

Tyler followed her and reached for her hand. "That's not what I'm talking about."

Beth shook her head. The look of resignation in her eyes bothered him more than the tears. "I'm sorry, Tyler. I never should've…" She swallowed hard, her gaze on the ground at her feet. "I can't do this." She took a step away from him. "I'm sorry."

"Can't do what? Beth, please tell me what's going on." He wanted to close the gap and pull her into his arms, but the look on her face suggested it wouldn't be welcomed. It was clear something had happened to her, and it went way beyond the interaction between her and the customer inside.

"Please, Tyler. Will you tell Monique that I'm not feeling well, and I'm going home?" Another tear escaped and slid down her cheek. She brushed it away.

"Of course."

She gave a sharp nod. "Thank you." A pause. "I really am sorry." And with that, she turned and hurried toward the exit.

Tyler was left standing there, a pit in his stomach. What just happened?

Chapter Twelve

Beth woke up Sunday morning with a raging headache. It was bad enough that it bordered on the beginning of a migraine. She forced herself to eat some breakfast and took medication to hold the migraine at bay. After that, she started water for a shower. She made it as hot as she could stand before stepping under the soothing spray.

It was no surprise she'd woken up feeling horrible. After beating herself up last night, on top of crying, she'd expected this. But it did feel a little like she was being kicked while she was down. She kept trying not to think about the day before. Everything was a disaster. Humiliating. She'd thought it would be horrible to tell Tyler about Carl and what he'd done, but in some ways, this was almost worse.

The way she reacted to her customer was bad enough, but for Tyler to witness her jumpy reaction... And then he'd been such a gentleman, too, following her to make sure she was all right.

Beth groaned, squeezed her eyes shut tight, and

turned her face to the water.

Tyler had been great. Everything in her being had wanted him to hold her and to assure her that all would be okay. But what would he have said when he found out how long it took her to leave Carl? Would there have been pity and sadness in his eyes every time he looked at her after that? She didn't think she could bear it. Instead, she'd left. Real mature move there.

She'd probably be crying again, but the tears were spent. Tyler was one of the best things that'd happened to her in a long time, and she'd blown it. He was probably questioning her sanity right now, and she couldn't blame him.

She turned again, allowing the water to pelt against her back, and wiped her face with a washcloth. She refused to leave the shower stall until the hot water disappeared and forced her out. The moment she slid the glass door open, real life waited for her like the cool air that hit her damp skin. Her cell phone lay on the bathroom counter, the green light on the top announcing she'd received a text.

Beth wrapped a towel around her hair and another around her body. She picked up the phone and swiped the screen to see a text from Tyler appear.

"I wanted to check in and see how you were doing. Let me know if you need anything, okay?"

Even an apparent mental breakdown of sorts hadn't kept him away. She wasn't real sure what to do with that information. Her heart soared with his thoughtfulness while her stomach rolled. She'd hoped to avoid talking about Carl for a while longer, but that wasn't going to fly now. Not if she were to keep seeing Tyler. Her heart ached in protest as she simply typed out, "I'm okay. Thank you."

How bad was it that she'd lied by text a half hour before going to church?

~

Tyler tossed his phone onto the kitchen counter with a sigh. It'd been three days since the incident at the zoo. Except for saying she was okay on Sunday, he hadn't heard from Beth. He certainly didn't feel comfortable continuing to send texts she wasn't responding to. He'd tried calling once, only to be sent to voicemail.

"Still nothing?" Dad's sympathetic expression did little to make Tyler feel better.

"Not a word. After what I saw happen, I told myself to not take her reaction personally, but it's getting harder to convince myself of that." He motioned toward the living room where Meg was watching a cartoon. "Beth promised she'd come to Meg's birthday party. Meg will be crushed if she isn't there."

Tyler had to admit to himself that he'd be upset with Beth if she didn't bother to swing by after making a promise. Calling and canceling would be one thing, but a no-show would break his daughter's heart.

"What are you going to do? Wait and see if she shows up?"

"I'd rather not find out at the last minute like that."

Dad nodded. "Maybe you need to talk to her in person."

Tyler didn't want to try and talk at the zoo, and going to her house was out of the question.

Or was it?

He knew where Beth lived. What if he tried to catch her at home on Thursday when she had the day off work? He'd rather look like a stalker and see her again than to keep wondering all week. "Yeah, maybe I will."

That night, Tyler had a hard time getting Meg settled and in bed. He pulled the pink and purple comforter up to her chin and brushed some of her dark hair out of her face. "You need to get some sleep, baby. You've got school tomorrow."

Meg made a face, her little nose scrunching in that adorable way that always made him smile. "I don't want to go to bed. I'm not tired." She reached up and rubbed her palms against his beard. "Don't ever shave, Daddy."

"You like my beard and mustache?" She nodded, and he smiled. "Thanks, baby. Me, too." He tapped her on the nose. "But you need to go to sleep. You'll be tired tomorrow." She didn't look convinced. "Besides, you need to save up energy for Saturday. You definitely don't want to be too tired for your party." He made an exaggerated sad face. "What if you're so tired you're cranky, then all your party guests see how grumpy you are and leave before cake and presents?" He tickled her then, soaking in her girly giggles.

"Daddy! I won't be cranky, I promise." She yawned, her eyelids lowering and lifting more slowly than they had a few minutes earlier.

"I believe you." He kissed her forehead. It was difficult to fathom that he only had this night and two more to tuck in a six-year-old. The thought caused his chest to tighten. His little girl was getting big way too fast. "If you can get to sleep and up in time tomorrow, we'll swing by and get pancakes before I take you to school. Does that sound good?"

Meg grinned and nodded. "Yay!"

"You ready to get some sleep?"

She pulled her giraffe to her and squeezed it tight. "Mr. Speckles and I are ready."

"Sleep good, baby. I love you."

"Love you, too, Daddy."

Tyler turned off her bedroom light and pulled the door closed behind him.

He wanted his little girl's birthday party to be perfect. If that meant going to Beth's house on Thursday and asking her directly if she was still coming or not, then that's exactly what he was going to do. He'd much rather Meg know ahead of time if one of her favorite people wasn't going to make it.

~

Beth spent an hour Thursday morning at the store combing through the toy aisles. Being a little girl herself at one time, she thought it'd be easy to choose a gift for Meg. She'd finally resorted to calling Miriam and asking for her opinion on the best toy to buy for a seven-year-old. With her purchase in a bag along with some wrapping paper and a big, purple bow, Beth got into her car and headed for home again.

Since she'd been dodging Tyler's call and texts, she probably wasn't welcome at Meg's birthday party, but she'd made a promise. At the very least, Beth wanted to buy the little girl a gift.

She parked in front of her apartment building and walked up the steps to her door. Tyler was the last person she expected to see standing against the brick wall, his hands in the pockets of his leather jacket. Beth stopped two steps away from the landing. "Hi."

"Hey."

She swallowed hard. How was it possible for him to look even more handsome with wind-tousled hair?

It'd only been a few days since they'd conversed regularly, and she'd missed him more than she'd thought possible. She'd missed looking forward to his random texts or listening to the sound of his voice. It'd been painful, but she'd been able to put up a wall—unstable though it may have been—while there'd been some distance between them. Could she maintain it now that he was standing right in front of her?

Tyler pushed away from the wall and took a step forward. "Can we talk for a few minutes?"

Beth ought to tell him no, make up an excuse for why she should run inside, or get back to her car again. The words wouldn't come. She only gave him a small nod and went to unlock her front door. She moved over to let him pass and tried to ignore the way his arm brushing hers sent tingles up and down her spine. After closing the door, she took in a deep breath. What was she supposed to say? "I've got juice and water if you'd like something to drink." Okay, well that could've been worse.

"Sure." Tyler looked about as unsure as she felt. "You want me to follow you or wait out here?"

"You can come into the kitchen."

Wordlessly, they headed that direction. She had a small island in the middle complete with two bar stools. She got a water out for herself and, after Tyler told her what he'd like, another for him. They sat down at the island. She'd never noticed how small the area was or how close the barstools were to each other until now. No matter where she put her legs, her knee kept brushing up against his.

Heat warmed her face. She cupped the ice-cold water bottle with both hands, desperately trying to absorb some of the coolness. "How are Meg and your dad doing?"

"They're good." He took a long drink of his water. "Meg was asking about you. She wondered if you were still coming to her birthday party, and I didn't know what to tell her." He pierced her with a guarded look that made it nearly impossible for Beth to figure out what he was thinking.

Beth nodded toward the bag she'd set down when they'd entered the kitchen. "I bought her birthday present." She paused. How was she supposed to ask her question? In the end, she decided straight forward was probably the best way. "I promised her, and I don't break my promises, but I wasn't sure if I should still go."

"Because of you, or because of me?"

She hadn't expected that question. All she could give him was a lame shrug.

"I'm confused, Beth. I thought things were going well with us." Tyler leaned forward with his elbow on the island. He ran his other hand through his hair. "I understand you were upset. What I don't get is why you're avoiding me."

How could she possibly explain things to him without going into what Carl had done? "What happened at work...it reminded me..." She paused for a deep breath and tried again. "It reminded me of the reasons I've avoided a relationship up until now. Why I shouldn't have let things between us go beyond friendship." Yeah, that sounded lame even to her own ears. She flinched when she saw the flash of hurt in his eyes.

"So that's it?" The hurt shifted to sadness and then anger. "Your ex. He hurt you, didn't he?"

Beth pushed away from the island and jumped to her feet. "If you'd rather I not come to the party, I can drop this by your house that morning. I definitely want Meg to know I'm thinking about her."

Tyler watched her for a few moments, clearly trying to decide whether to let her change the subject or bring their conversation back on track. "Meg would like you to be there, and so would I."

Waves of relief and nerves battled each other for top billing. "Okay."

"Okay." He released a deep sigh. "I care about you, Beth, and I wish you felt comfortable enough to talk to me about what happened." He took in her expression, and it looked like he was going to reach out to her. Instead, he shoved his hands into his pockets. "I hope you know that I'd never hurt you."

Beth nodded. She hated that she was making him worry about that. "I know."

Tyler walked to the front door and pulled it open. He turned before stepping past the threshold, and Beth, who was on his heels, ran right into him. She braced her hands against his chest to keep herself from bouncing off his solid frame. The feel of his muscles beneath her palms combined with the way his breath fluttered the hair around her face made Beth's heart race. "Sorry."

He gathered her hands in his. "Don't be. I like this. Us."

Beth's mouth went dry at the intensity in his dark eyes. Yeah, she liked this a whole lot, too. Way more than she should right now when she was trying to put a little space between them. She needed time to think; to get her tangled mess of emotions straightened out. His eyes lowered to her mouth, and she thought he was going to kiss her. Wanted him to. Or didn't. Ugh!

He must have sensed her uncertainty because he took a step back, her hands still in his. "I want you to take the time you need. The last thing I want to do is pressure you. But you should know I'm not going anywhere." Like the gentleman he was, he lifted one hand to his lips and placed a soft kiss against her knuckles. "Call if you want to talk. For the record, I'm a good listener." He gave her one last half-smile and slipped out of her place.

The galloping of her heart nearly drowned out the sound of the door closing behind him. She leaned against it and let the back of her head bang against the wood with a groan. "Why can't I just be normal?"

Chapter Thirteen

Tyler shouldn't be this relieved to see Beth walk through the door of the pizza place. Pressure lifted from his chest, and it felt like he could focus on making sure the rest of Meg's party went off without a hitch.

There was no missing when Meg spotted her, either. His now-seven-year-old jumped up from her small group of friends and raced across the dining area with a loud, "Beth!" echoing off the walls. Tyler tried not to flinch at her loud voice while simultaneously smiling at the way Meg threw herself at Beth. Beth didn't miss a beat. She held the gift bag in one hand while crouching down and gathering Meg in a hug with the other arm. Her smile as she spoke to Meg was genuine.

Boy, he'd missed that gorgeous smile. He'd given her space since he spoke with her on Thursday, and he planned to continue to do so. At the same time, his cell phone never left his side. He wasn't about to admit how often he glanced at it, hoping for a call or text from her.

For now, he'd enjoy being in the same room with her and hope she felt the same.

Beth and Meg walked back, hand-in-hand. Beth waved and said hello to Dad and then her gaze collided with Tyler's. The corners of her mouth pulled up a little. "Hi."

"Hi. I'm glad you could make it."

"Oh, me, too!" Meg flopped down on the empty chair next to her friends. "This is my favorite place to eat in the whole wide world. It's even better than ice cream. Or at least just as good as it." She then proceeded to introduce her five friends to Beth. "She's the one who came with the zoo animals? Do you remember?" There was no missing the pride on the girl's face, and the other kids seemed appropriately impressed.

Meg turned back to Beth. "Do you know what kind of pizza I like best?"

"What kind?" Beth covered an amused laugh.

"I like double cheese with sausage. I could eat a whole pizza all by myself!"

Beth set the gift bag on the table next to the others. "Well, since you're seven now, I bet you'll be able to eat even more. Of course, I hear there's going to be cake. You want to save room for that, right?"

Meg put both hands on her stomach and puffed it out. "I've *always* got room for cake." She turned to Tyler. "Daddy, can we have the tokens for some games now? Please?"

Tyler reached for the cups of tokens he'd bought for tonight. It ought to keep the kids busy for at least fifteen minutes. He chuckled. "Sure, baby." He handed a cup to each child. "Remember, that's all there is. Use them wisely."

"Yippee! Call us when the pizza gets here!"

Meg and her friends ran off, leaving the adults behind.

Dad leaned back in his chair. "That girl gives me a real run for my money." He motioned to another chair. "Have a seat, Beth. Thanks for coming. As Meg kept telling us, the party couldn't start until you got here."

Beth sat down and continued to watch Meg laugh with a friend as she threw balls in the skeet game. "It's nice the gaming area is open enough so you see almost everything from here."

Tyler nodded. "Yep, one of my favorite things about this place." He lowered his voice. "They don't have the best pizza in town, but sometimes it's not all about the food."

"Very true." She tucked some wayward strands of hair behind her ear. Her hair was weaved into a braid that hung down her back and reflected the light from the bulbs overhead.

He cleared his throat. "I ordered sausage and pepperoni. I hope that's okay. If you prefer a different kind of pizza, please let me know, and I'll be happy to add to the order."

"No, that's fine. The only pizza I can't stand is macaroni and cheese." She shuddered. "There are limits to what should be put on a pizza." They all laughed. Beth looked around the dining area. "I take it this is a drop off party?"

"It didn't begin that way, but apparently that's becoming the norm. I'm glad I limited her to inviting five friends." Tyler would have preferred a parent stay and decided to make that a note on the invitation next year. He made sure Meg was still where he could see her and sat down in the chair across the table from Dad and Beth. It'd be easier to hear them both that way. The fact that he could see Beth better, too, had little to do with it. He almost rolled his eyes at himself for his wayward train of thought.

"Five friends is nice. I never cared much for the big parties as a kid." Beth looked thoughtful as she picked at the corner of one of her thumbs. "I had one with a number of classmates in kindergarten. It was completely overwhelming. After that, it was either family only, or I invited one friend to celebrate with me, and I was fine with that."

Dad nodded. "There's nothing wrong with that."

Tyler listened to her voice as she and Dad visited until Dad pointed behind Tyler.

He turned and saw someone coming with a pizza balanced on each hand. They didn't even have to call the kids because they'd come running back and were sitting in their chairs again before the pizzas were on the table. It didn't escape his notice that Meg had chosen the chair next to Beth.

"Yay!" Meg smiled up at the guy who brought it. "Thank you."

That brought a grin to his face. "You're welcome. Happy birthday and enjoy the pizza."

Beth nudged Meg. "So how many tickets did you get from the games?"

Meg dug into her little pockets and pulled out a wad of orange paper. "I might have enough to get one of the pink frogs. It even has a tiara." She pointed to the pizza. "Can I have that piece with the extra sausage please?"

Tyler laughed. That was his daughter: Blink and

you'll miss the change in topic. "Yes, baby. You sure can." He served the kids, amazed at how quickly they could devour their food considering they were talking half the time. He couldn't take his eyes off how Meg and Beth were interacting.

Meg grinned, a string of cheese hanging out the corner of her mouth, as she leaned into Beth. In turn, Beth gave the girl a big hug, said something in a whisper, and had Meg giggling.

Dad gave Tyler a knowing look, and his heart squeezed. *God, please keep Beth in our lives. If not for me, then for Meg.*

As they ate pizza, Meg kept eyeing her birthday gifts. When they finished, Tyler figured he may as well end her suffering. "Would you like to open presents now? Or wait until after the cake?"

Meg clasped her hands in front of her. "Oh! Open them now!"

Tyler chuckled, as if he had any doubt how Meg was going to answer that question. She opened all the presents from her friends before she took a gift bag from her Grandpa. She reached in and pulled out a little hat, jacket, and shoes. The gift clearly confused her.

"There's something else in there, too." Dad waited until she found a brightly colored shirt. "They're for Mr. Speckles."

Meg grinned as she looked the miniature clothing over with renewed enthusiasm. "These are great, Grandpa. Mr. Speckles is going to love them, thank you!"

Beth shot Tyler a questioning look.

"Mr. Speckles is her plush giraffe."

"Of course." Beth didn't miss a beat. "I'm sure

he'll look quite handsome in his new outfit."

Meg put the clothing back in the bag and reached for the one Beth brought. Tyler noticed Beth sit up straight and look a little nervous. She shouldn't have, though, because Meg squealed with joy as she withdrew a set of My Little Ponies. "I've wanted some of these. How did you know?"

Beth shrugged. "It was a lucky guess." She winked at her. "You might want to look in there and make sure you got everything."

Meg set the ponies on the table and peered inside the purple bag. She pulled a book out with an adorable little girl giving a zebra a hug. The illustration was as beautiful as it was eye catching. Meg studied the title: *Zoe the Zebra to the Rescue.*

That's when Tyler noticed the author's name: Elizabeth Davenport. His heart swelled with pride. She'd done it, and from what he could see of the book, it looked as good or better than any book he'd bought Meg at the bookstore or online. "Did you see that, Meg? Beth wrote that book."

His daughter's mouth formed an "o" as she stared at the cover. "You wrote this? Wow." She thumbed through the first three pages. "I can't wait to read it!"

Beth looked relieved. "I'm glad, Meg. Will you do me a favor? After you read it, I want you to tell me what you think about it, okay? Do you promise?"

Meg nodded. "I promise. Thank you, Beth!"

"You're welcome, sweetie."

Tyler slid the last gift across the table to Meg and watched as she found her way through the wrapping paper.

"My ballet dress! You got it!" Beth jumped out

of her chair and held the purple dress in front of her. "It's so pretty. Thank you, Daddy." She oohed and ahhed over the slippers and a variety of hair accessories he'd found to go with it.

"You're welcome, Meg. Happy birthday, baby."

Meg grinned as she and her friends went through and admired all the gifts.

Tyler took that moment to look across the table at Beth and mouth, "I'm proud of you."

A little smile graced her face, and the whole dining area seemed brighter.

~

Beth had gone to Meg's birthday party nervous and uncertain. She'd had fun celebrating with laughter, the pizza, and cake. Not only that, but Meg had truly seemed to love the book. Beth had relived that moment multiple times, and she wasn't sure which part meant the most to her: That Meg had been excited to read the book, or that Tyler said he was proud of her.

She'd gone in not knowing what to expect, but they'd all treated her like one of them. Like family. She pictured herself spending other events with them. An image of Beth and Tyler toasting in the new year, shortly followed by a toe-curling kiss that didn't seem to end, had her stomach doing cartwheels.

She swallowed and tried to re-focus her attention on the Christmas tree she was helping her parents decorate.

"Here, Bethie. Take this one." Mom handed her one of the crocheted trees with jingle bells sewed all over it. "I remember when you made that. You were what? Seven or eight?"

Beth chuckled as the sad little tree sagged when she hung it up. Mom always did love all the little ornaments that she and her siblings had made by hand over the years. Truthfully, some of them should probably be thrown away. Like the Santa made from clay whose eyes, nose, and even hat had fallen off at some point in the past.

"Thanks, Mom." She found a spot on the tree to hang it. It was tradition for her to come over and help her parents decorate their tree. It wasn't that Beth didn't enjoy decorating for Christmas. Since it was just her in her little apartment, she simply chose not to put up a tree. She hung pictures, added a centerpiece to the island, and her place always smelled like apples and cinnamon. Putting up a tree seemed like a lot of work, especially when she spent a good deal of her time either here or at Avalon's house during this time of the year anyway.

Dad held an ornament depicting two angels kissing. "I remember when I gave this to your mother the first Christmas we were married." His hand shook a little and then he turned to accept a kiss from his wife.

"It was the sweetest thing." Mom reached out and touched the ornament with her finger.

Beth smiled and turned to find another ornament to hang. Her parents certainly had their disagreements over the years, but their love for each other always prevailed. Beth grew up hoping to find someone like that to share her life with. What if Tyler could be that someone? Her thoughts surprised her, and she stopped in the middle of hanging an ornament.

He said he cared about her, but what did that mean? What if she let herself fall for him and then he never felt the same way?

What if she spent the rest of her life alone?

Mom carefully placed the pieces of a glass nativity set on the mantle above the fireplace. "We were wondering if you'd like to spend the night Christmas Eve. With Marian and her family here, it might be fun. Or I'm sure you could stay with Avalon and Gwen over there."

Who was Beth kidding? She'd never be alone in her life, not with all her family around her, and that gave her a measure of peace. The thought of waking up at one house or the other and getting to see nieces and nephews discover the contents of their stockings sounded like fun. "Sure, Mom. I'd like that. Why don't I stay with Avalon? It'll give you guys a little more room here."

They'd need it. With Marian's large family, she and Jason and the baby would probably sleep in one room, and then they'd split the other three kids up one way or another. Beth would be sleeping on the couch in either home, and thought that it might be easier over at Avalon's.

Mom seemed happy with that. "Wonderful. Don't forget to mention it to your sister."

Dad patted Beth on the arm and they continued to decorate the tree.

At one point, they took a break for Dad to rest. Beth followed her mom into the kitchen to get all of them something to drink.

Beth got the glasses out while Mom found the eggnog in the fridge. "Are you going to invite Tyler and his family over for Christmas?"

One of the glasses slipped from Beth's hand and she managed to catch it before it hit the counter. She set it down quickly. "Aren't we having it over at the

Chandler house? I'm not about to invite more guests over there. That's not my place." Lexi's mom, Patty, had offered to host last Beth heard.

Mom took a drink of her eggnog and then filled the cup again before putting the carton back in the fridge. "Patty and I were talking. We decided that, with Marian and Jason coming with all the kids, it might be easier to do it here." She lowered her voice. "I thought it might be less stressful for your dad, too."

Beth nodded. "I can see that." It probably would be easier on Dad to be here in his own house. He wouldn't admit it, though.

"Since it'll be here, you should invite Tyler. Meg would fit right in with the passel of kids we'll have. Your dad and Bill seemed to get along well at his birthday party."

Beth couldn't deny the truth in that, either. But after the weirdness this last week, how was she supposed to call Tyler up and ask him over to spend Christmas with her? She must have hesitated long enough to earn Mom's patented, "Okay, what're you hiding?" look. Beth had hoped to avoid this conversation.

"I'm not sure what's going to happen between me and Tyler, Mom." She'd love to leave it there, but there was no way that she'd get away with it. She took a sip of eggnog and told Mom about the scene at the gift shop. "I know my reaction was exaggerated, but it is what it is. I went to Meg's birthday party earlier this evening, and they were all nice to me." Beth's voice caught. "I dug myself into a hole, and I'm not real sure how to get back out of it again."

Mom pulled her into a tight hug. "Bethie, you need to tell him what happened. Explain why you reacted the way you did."

Beth winced, and her stomach lurched. "And if he feels sorry for me? Or even worse, thinks I'm crazy?"

"Then he isn't worth your time." Mom slipped an arm around Beth's shoulders. "Your daddy and I are praying for you. Any man worth his salt will not define you by what happened to you in the past, he'll love you for who you are." She handed Beth her glass of eggnog. "Come on, let's go finish putting that tree up, hmmm?"

"Yeah." Beth followed her into the living room. She went through the motions, but her mind was somewhere else entirely. Mom's words kept echoing in her head. *He'll love you for who you are.*

If only that were true. If only she could know what the future held, then maybe she wouldn't keep pushing him away. It was obvious Tyler liked her. Cared about her even. But loved her? She wasn't sure about that. Seriously, here she was an emotional mess. It was clear Tyler knew something had happened to her, yet she wasn't telling him. If positions were reverse, she'd sure wonder what he was hiding. Beth frowned.

What was Tyler doing right now? Meg was probably playing with the new toys she got at her birthday party. Picturing the little girl brought a smile to Beth's face. Mom was right, Meg would love spending Christmas here with all of Beth's nieces and nephews.

What am I supposed to do, God? I don't want to get hurt again. You're going to have to give me an opening and the words to tell Tyler about what happened, because I don't think I have the strength to do it on my own.

Chapter Fourteen

Tyler sat next to Meg and listened as she explained the difference between the three My Little Ponies she'd received from Beth the day before. She had each of them memorized down to the shade of pink in their hair.

Beth did well choosing gifts. Meg read through Beth's book three or four times that he knew of. He'd read it, too. Not only was the story engaging and sweet, but it taught a valuable lesson. The illustrator Beth hired had only added to the tale. He had no doubt her book would do well once it was released.

"You know what, Daddy? I think I'm going to ask Santa for Rainbow Dash. That pony is pretty with all the different colors. I wonder if it's too late to send a letter to Santa and add it to my wish list."

Considering Christmas Eve was two weeks from today, probably so. "You can send him a letter, but don't be surprised if you don't get it. It is pretty late in the game."

Meg finished her chicken nugget and nodded.

"Yeah, that's what I thought."

They were eating lunch in one of the local fast food places. Dad had awakened with a cough and didn't feel well. Tyler thought he'd take Meg out for lunch after church, that way Dad could get a nap while the house was quiet. Tyler insisted Meg eat all her nuggets and fries before going to play on the indoor playground.

His daughter paused, her fry halfway between the ketchup in front of her and her mouth. "Laura's here!"

"Laura?" He twisted and caught sight of Avalon and her daughter. He chuckled. "Lorelei, baby." He waved, and Avalon headed their way, her daughter on one hip and a tray of food in the opposite hand.

"Hi, guys!" Avalon smiled, set the tray down on the next table over, then turned her attention to Meg. "Happy late birthday. I heard you had a fun party."

Meg crammed the fry in her mouth, chewed at light speed, and swallowed. "I did! It was so much fun. And did Beth tell you she came to my party and brought me some My Little Ponies and one of her books? If I'd known you'd be here, I'd have bringed them to show you. I'll bet Laura would like it." She paused, her brows pinched together. "Laura-lie."

"I wish we could see them. Maybe we'll get to one day."

Her comment surprised Tyler a little but Avalon didn't seem to think anything of it as she placed Lorelei in a high chair and handed her a chicken nugget. Once her daughter was all set up, Avalon collapsed onto the bench and released a sigh. "Duke had to go into the ranch and work this afternoon. Since it's chilly today, it seemed like a good idea to come here." She looked around at the busy dining area. "Obviously my idea was less than original."

"This is a popular place," he agreed. He pointed toward Meg's food. "Don't forget to eat."

Meg had been watching Lorelai. "It's okay, Daddy. I want to wait until Laura-lie is done eating so we can go play together."

Avalon's phone rang. By the bits of conversation Tyler heard, he assumed it was probably Duke on the other end of the call. She hung up right before the girls were done with their lunches. Avalon cleaned Lorelei up, set her down, and chuckled as the girls ran together to the play area. "Meg's great with her."

Tyler watched as Meg helped Lorelei climb the little slide and then waited for the toddler to slide back down again. "She talked about your daughter for days after Thanksgiving. We had a great time with your whole family."

"We're glad you could join us." She took a bite of her salad thoughtfully. "I'm also happy to hear that my sister made it to Meg's birthday party." She gave him a knowing look.

"Me, too." He didn't know Avalon well enough to talk about Beth. He wondered, though, if Beth had said anything about what was going on. He cleared his throat. "Meg's gotten real attached to her." She wasn't the only one, but he wasn't going to admit that to someone he barely knew.

Avalon seemed to be gauging whether she should say something or not. "Do me a favor and don't give up on Beth, okay?"

Tyler's brows lifted. He hadn't expected her to say anything quite that obvious. "She doesn't make it easy when she keeps dodging me and won't return my calls."

Avalon wrinkled her nose a little. "She's got a lot of self-confidence issues. Her ex was a real messed up guy. Look, it's not my place to give you details. That's up to Beth. But he was abusive, and she has a real reason for hesitating when it comes to another relationship. You're good for her, we all saw it at Thanksgiving."

He hadn't thought Avalon could surprise him more until now. He suddenly wanted to know exactly what her family said. What made them think he was good for her when Beth herself clearly did not? Doubts assailed him like they had all week. He'd been wondering whether he should call Lexi and cancel his promise to volunteer at the hospital on Saturday. Or at least see if she could swap him to a different station so that he wasn't pushing his luck with Beth. If she was trying to avoid him, he certainly didn't want to keep pressing the issue.

If Beth was going to walk away, maybe it was best to cut ties before things got too involved.

It was too late, though. No matter what happened with Beth, she held a piece of his heart in her hands.

Tyler barely noticed when Avalon got up and went to help Lorelei with something. He stared out the window as cars went through the drive-through line. His heart hammered in his chest, and he straightened his spine with the realization that he was in love with Beth. A messy, no holds barred, real love that he'd never experienced before.

How was it possible to feel both peace and a sense of urgency at the same time? *All right, God. I have no idea what I'm supposed to do next.*

One thing was certain: Beth didn't trust him. At

least not enough to tell him about her ex and share why she was pulling away. Maybe that's what he needed to focus on. He needed to gain her trust and prove that he'd be there for her no matter what.

Avalon was right. He had to do everything he could to show Beth he wasn't giving up on her.

~

"What's up, big brother?" Beth entered Davenport Cabinetry and closed the door behind her. It was her day off, and Lance had sent her a text asking her to swing by when she was free. She'd spent the morning helping the hospital committee decorate the building for Christmas followed by a lunch provided for all the volunteers. This was the last stop before she got home and collapsed from exhaustion.

"Hey, there you are. Everything go okay this morning? Lexi was worried since they usually decorate the hospital before now." Lance set his tools down and stood.

Beth knew Lexi had wanted to be there today. Her job as a nurse for one of the local pediatricians didn't allow for it, though. "Oh yeah, the lobby looks great. We should be good to go for this weekend."

Lance shuffled through some papers on the desk until he found what he was looking for. "Lexi gave this to me. It's instructions for Operation: Joy on Saturday." He paused. "For Tyler."

She took the paper from him and stared at it. "Okay. Why didn't she leave it at the hospital for him to get when he arrived?" Beth wasn't even sure he was still going to show up to help her deliver cookies. Did she want him to? Yes. *Should* she want him to? That question brought up another whole mess of emotions she didn't want to examine right now.

At least her brother had the good sense to look contrite. He knew as well as Beth did that this was an excuse to try and get her to talk to Tyler. Between this and the hints Avalon was throwing around in a not-so-subtle way, Beth had gotten the picture. Her family liked Tyler. Well, she did too. If only things didn't have to be so complicated. "I'll make sure he gets it, thanks." She folded it into quarters and slipped it into her back pocket. "Any news on the adoption front?"

"Actually, yeah." Lance pulled his cell phone out, a big grin on his face. "I'm trying to not get attached, but it's hard. The birth mom, Kate, hadn't wanted to know whether the baby was a boy or a girl. She's measuring a little small and had an ultrasound to make sure everything's fine and invited us to be there. The baby's perfectly healthy."

He showed her an ultrasound that was clearly the baby's profile. Beth could make out the little nose and even the lips. "Oh my goodness. Talk about adorable!" She touched the little face with a finger and then handed the phone back to him.

"After taking a few measurements, Kate asked us if we wanted to know the sex of the baby. We jumped at the chance." He paused for dramatic effect. "It's a boy."

Tears sprang to Beth's eyes before he'd even finished his sentence. She threw her arms around Lance's neck. "You're going to have a son."

He nodded. "Lex and I are trying hard to keep some emotional distance in case the same thing happens this time. But when I saw this ultrasound picture," he held the phone up for emphasis, "I felt peace, and I knew that was our child."

"I'm happy for you both." She swiped a tear away and smiled as she took a step back. "You two deserve this. Did you tell everyone yet?"

"The little guy's not due until the first week in January. We're going to tell everyone about him at Christmas. Since both of our families will be together, we thought it'd be fun."

"I have no idea how you're keeping this a secret, but I think that'll be the best Christmas present of all." Beth quickly held up two fingers. "And no one will hear a thing from me. Scout's honor. If you need anything, let me know, okay?"

"Will do." He picked up a pencil and his level. "I'd better get back to this. Will you do me one favor?"

"What's that?"

"Go talk to your mechanic."

Beth rolled her eyes. "Avalon put you up to that, didn't she?"

"Maybe. But I think it'll be a mistake if you let fear guide you. You deserve better than that." His serious expression shifted, and he nodded toward the door. "Go on and get out of my hair. I'll talk to you soon."

"Alright. Love you!"

"Love you, too."

Beth drove home, her heart lighter than it had been in a long time. She couldn't wait to see the faces of their family members when Lance and Lexi told everyone the good news.

She walked up to her front door and noticed a bouquet of flowers sitting on the ground nearby. It was an arrangement of cheerful white daisies and gorgeous blue forget-me-nots. Beth picked them up, unlocked the door, and carried them inside. The subtle fragrance of the flowers tickled her nose. She breathed deeply and withdrew the small card.

"Beth,
These flowers made me think of your bright smile, blue eyes, and beautiful spirit. I miss seeing you.
Fondly,
Tyler"

Beth read the card twice more. It was one of the sweetest things anyone had ever said to her. She ran a thumb over the hand-written note. She missed him, too. Way more than she'd even admitted to herself.

Beth remembered the note in her pocket. After changing into a shirt without holiday paint and glitter on it, she got in her car and headed over to Martin Mechanics.

There was no one in the office when she arrived. Rather than ring the bell, she opted to walk around the side to the garage itself since it didn't seem busy. A sound from the other side of an old Ford pickup caught her attention. Unsure whether it was Bill or Tyler, she picked her way across the garage. Right before she reached the truck, Tyler stepped into view, his eyes widening. "I'm sorry if I didn't hear the bell." He jabbed a thumb toward the office.

"I just came in, I hope that's okay."

"Of course." He wiped his palms against the legs of his jeans adding to the streaks of oil already there. He wore a long-sleeved, button-up shirt with the Martin Mechanic's logo on it with the sleeves rolled all the way up to his biceps.

Beth's throat suddenly went dry. No man should

look this good in work clothes and oil. He was watching her, waiting for her to tell him why she'd come by. There was curiosity, a little humor, and something else in his eyes. She cleared her throat. "I got the flowers you sent. They're beautiful, thank you."

"You're welcome. I'm glad you like them." He reached a hand out. "You've got some glitter in your hair."

"Oh!" She moved to brush it away at the same time he did, their hands hitting each other. She gathered her hair together and shook it a little, hoping to dislodge the shiny pieces. "I helped the hospital volunteer committee decorate this morning. I'll probably be finding glitter for a week." When she chuckled, it sounded nervous even to her own ears. *Great, Beth. You sound like an idiot.* Then she remembered the paper. "Lexi wanted me to give this to you. It has some of the directions for Saturday night." He took the paper from her. "I wasn't sure if you were still going to be there or not."

Tyler had been reading the paper, but his head lifted quickly at her words. "I was planning on it, unless you'd rather I didn't."

It was impossible to tell what kind of response he was hoping for.

Beth shook her head. "No. I mean, I'm glad you're still going."

There was no missing the relief on his face, quickly replaced with a smile. "Good." He refolded the paper and put it in a pocket. "I'm not supposed to dress up like an elf or anything like that, right?"

She pictured him in costume and cracked up. "Something festive like a red shirt will be fine. But you can get as fancy as you want. Keep in mind we're carrying cookies around: There will be frosting."

"Sounds like fun."

They were both silent for several moments. Beth shuffled her feet and kicked at an invisible spot on the concrete. "I guess I should go and let you work. Looks like it's just you today, huh?"

"Dad wasn't feeling well earlier this week. After some serious effort on my part, I got him to promise to rest one more day before coming back to work tomorrow." He paused. "Where are you headed to next?"

To my lonely apartment where I'll watch re-runs and probably eat a can of soup. Yeah, that sounds like fun. "I figured I'd go home and put my feet up for a while." She self-consciously tucked some hair behind one ear.

"If you're not in a hurry, you're welcome to stay. I'd love some company. I even have some cold sodas in the fridge."

Beth found herself agreeing. He brought a chair in from the office for her. Then he retrieved her favorite soda and handed it to her with a hopeful smile effectively sending warmth traveling through her body from head to toe.

Chapter Fifteen

Tyler loosened a bolt until he could work it out with his hands. He'd always prided himself in his ability to focus on a job and get it done. Until now. At this moment, it took all his effort to keep his attention on what was in front of him instead of the pretty woman sitting in the chair nearby. That Beth had agreed to stay was huge. If it weren't for the fact that Dad was out, and they were behind a little this week, Tyler would've stopped working and visited with her for a while.

"What made you decide to become a mechanic? I'm assuming watching your dad had some influence on it."

Beth's soft voice flowed over Tyler like warm honey. He glanced at her and enjoyed the way her hair perfectly framed her face.

"That was definitely part of it. I always liked puzzles, even as a kid. I don't know how many things I tore apart and put back together again. I know it drove my mom crazy, although she never told me I couldn't do it."

"Did they work once they were put back together?"

"Every time." He paused. "More or less."

Their laughter mingled. Beth's perfume competed with the normal smell of the garage, something Tyler could easily get used to.

He turned back to the engine he was working on. "What about you? I can tell you enjoy your work at the zoo. Is that what you've always wanted to do?" The delay in her response brought his full attention back to her face. She seemed to be struggling with whether she should speak her mind or not. Tyler held his breath, praying she'd open up to him a little.

"My job at the zoo is great. Especially if they'll let me help with the summer classes next year. But mostly, it's a job that pays the bills and doesn't take up my evenings. That way I have plenty of time to write."

"That's awesome. "You're great with kids and seem to really get them. You've got a real talent, Beth. I'm serious, the book you gave Meg is great." He continued to work as they talked. "What made you decide to publish independently?"

"I tried the traditional route with a few pieces, but it didn't pan out. I found a great group online I've been involved in that helps support the idea of publishing my books on my own. I'm going to focus on writing books for kids around Meg's age. I like the idea of snagging the interest of a new reader and writing that first chapter book they ever read." Beth's eyes lit up as she talked, completely mesmerizing Tyler. She was passionate about this subject, and he found that made her even more attractive. She flashed him a shy smile and motioned to the truck he was working on. "What exactly are you doing to this poor thing?"

Tyler beckoned her over. "Let me show you."

He spent the next ten or fifteen minutes illustrating what he was doing to repair the engine. Beth seemed interested as she stood over the engine and even leaned in to see what he was talking about. Her hair brushed against his face as the scent of her shampoo enveloped him. When she looked at him again, they were so close, it would only take a small movement on his part to kiss her. His gaze shifted from her eyes, vulnerable and questioning, to her lips then back again. Every fiber in his being wanted to take her in his arms. It'd been way too long since the last time he'd tasted her sweet lips. She'd opened up to him some today, and the last thing he wanted was to rush things. Instead, he hooked some of her soft hair with one finger, deposited it behind her ear with a smile, and finished telling her about the motor.

When she headed home almost an hour later, Tyler's hope for a future with her was bolstered. The event at the hospital was only a couple days away, and he couldn't wait to see her again.

~

Beth smoothed the skirt of her green dress that fell to an inch or two below her knees, the silky fabric smooth and cool to the touch. It'd been cold walking into the hospital. She shivered in the black sweater she'd brought, thankful she'd chosen to wear tights instead of nylons to help keep her legs warm. The whole hospital was heated, and once she started delivering plates of goodies, she wouldn't need her sweater anymore. But for now, she tugged it closed in front of her and suppressed another shiver.

The huge conference room was bustling with activity as volunteers gathered. Many of them had been at the hospital for hours cooking meals, getting the plates of cookies together, and compiling lists of patients along with what would be delivered to their rooms. The person dressing up as Santa Claus this year was probably up in the children's ward making his round to see the kids who couldn't leave their rooms or beds. Later, he'd be down in the cafeteria to listen to the wishes of the rest of the children.

Beth hugged herself, tears pricking her eyelids as she observed the large number of people who were giving their time to make tonight a success. It may only be a few hours out of their day, but it was a bright light in what was a stressful time in many of these patients' lives.

"Are you cold?"

Tyler's voice behind her brought a smile to her face. She blinked away the tears as she turned toward him. "A little. I think they're expecting a freeze overnight."

"I don't doubt it." His gaze went to the green Santa hat on her head and traveled all the way down to her feet before focusing on her face again. "You look amazing. Seriously, you're festive and cute and pretty all at the same time. How did you manage that?"

Her heart pranced against her ribs. She was glad she'd chosen green, since she blushed often enough without having red to accentuate it. "Thank you." She motioned to the Christmas light necklace that matched her earrings. "And for the kids…" With a flip of a switch, they started blinking.

"Brilliant."

Yeah, about like that million-dollar smile of his. Between it, the black slacks, and the button-up red plaid shirt, Tyler looked like he'd stepped right out of a Christmas catalog. "You don't look half-bad yourself, mister."

His grin widened, and he offered her his arm. "Shall we figure out where we're supposed to be?"

Once she looped her arm through his, he placed a hand on hers. All remnants of the chilly weather outside disappeared, and it was all Beth could do to not give in and lean into his warmth.

They got inside and gathered with the other volunteers. One of the co-chairs of the committee clapped his hands and got everyone's attention. "Thank you all for coming. As you know, this is the tenth year we've carried out Operation: Joy here at Kitner Memorial Hospital. While there are some wonderful reasons to be at the hospital—such as the birth of a new member of the family—many of the patients are here for less joyous reasons. As you deliver goodies, please keep that in mind. Be sensitive, give space when needed or asked, and be mindful of the lists we give you. What you are doing today matters, and for some of the patients in our care, this may be the highlight of their holiday season." He grinned and made a "shooing" motion with his hands. "Now go spread some of that Christmas joy!"

The volunteers cheered, Beth and Tyler included. Good grief, she was blinking tears away for the second time tonight and the evening hadn't even started. This event always made her emotional anyway. She sniffed discretely as the volunteers milled about.

"Any idea where we're supposed to go?"

She turned to find Tyler looking at the paper

she'd given him the other day. "Follow me."

Before long, they had a cart loaded with plates of goodies and a list of which fourth-floor hospital rooms they were delivering them to. In the elevator on the way up, Beth shrugged off her sweater and stashed it in the bottom of the cart. "You ready for this?"

Tyler flashed her a grin. "You bet."

They took plates of cookies and candy to many hospital rooms. Some of the occupants smiled in anticipation of their arrival. Others were more somber, and a few patients were even sleeping so Beth and Tyler left the treats on a table or with the nurse.

About halfway through the second cart of plates, they came to a hospital room where a young girl was sitting on the edge of a hospital bed. A woman Beth assumed was the girl's mother slept, several tubes and wires attached to her pale frame. The moment they entered the room, the girl carefully eased herself off the bed and came over to them, her eyes wide. Beth thought she couldn't be any older than ten.

"Mama's asleep. My dad went to go get some more coffee, but he should be right back." Her eyes flicked to the plate of goodies in Tyler's hands. "Is that for us?"

Tyler gave her a kind smile. "It is." He handed the plate to her. "Now you have to share, no eating all of that yourself."

That lifted the corners of the girl's mouth up a little. She nodded, her ponytail bouncing. "Don't worry, I'll share. Besides, I see a frosted cookie with sprinkles in there. I'm going to save that one for Mama." Her face fell again. "She's got pneumonia. I really, really hope she gets to come home again in time for Christmas."

Footsteps in the doorway announced the arrival of a man Beth assumed to be the girl's father. He shifted a cup of coffee to his left and shook hands with Tyler. "Real nice of you folks to do this. Celia could use a little cheering up today."

"Look, Daddy! Did you see all these cookies? We should eat some, don't you think?" Celia tilted the plate to show her father the goodies.

"They do look good. I'm sure we can have a few." He winked at his daughter.

Celia set the plate down on one of the little tables in the room and turned back toward Beth. "I like your necklace. Have you tried it in the dark yet?"

Before anyone could say a word, she'd turned off the lights in the room. Beth's necklace glowed and blinked, casting cheerful holiday colors on the walls and ceilings. Light from the hallway illuminated Celia's face enough for Beth to see the wonder in her eyes.

Without thinking about it, Beth lifted the necklace off and placed it around the girl's neck. Celia looked down at it, gently fingering one of the glowing bulbs. "I can keep this?" Her gaze lifted, and the hope there made Beth wish she had a hundred more necklaces to give away.

"Absolutely. It's all yours."

"Thank you!" Celia bounced over to her father. "Look! Then when Mama wakes up, she'll have Christmas lights all around her." She flipped the room's lights back on again and flopped into a chair by the bed.

Her father cleared his throat. "Thank you both. It's been a rough week, but Lisa's fever broke this afternoon. The doctors think, if all goes well, she'll be back home in a few days."

"That's wonderful." Tyler put an arm around Beth and gave her a squeeze. "We'll be keeping Lisa and your whole family in our prayers."

"I appreciate that."

Beth followed Tyler out of the room. It wasn't until they'd reached the end of the hallway that she sagged against the wall. "Makes you appreciate how fortunate we are, doesn't it?"

"It sure does." He shifted closer to her, his arm brushing against hers. "You were amazing back there."

For delivering cookies? Compared to the people that organized this whole thing, or the individuals fighting for their health and lives, Beth had done very little. "I hope we gave some people a reason to smile tonight."

"You did more than that for Celia." He gently bumped her shoulder with his. "I'm proud to be here with you."

His words and the way he grinned made Beth chuckle. Their gazes locked and something in his eyes caused her breath to hitch.

"Are you two going to bring goodies in sometime today?" The older voice held a note of amusement.

Only then did Beth notice they were standing directly outside another hospital room. An older woman lay on the bed, blankets pulled up to her chest. The smile on her face lit up her eyes and made the rest of the machines in the room fade away. "This old woman's been waiting all evening for her plate of goodies." Her laughter told them she was joking and enjoying herself.

Tyler smiled. "Are you a baked goods or candy kind of gal?"

"Baked goods, young man."

He lifted a plate from the cart. "In that case, we

present you with extra cookies, light on the candy." Tyler handed it to her with a flourish.

The older woman studied the contents, nodded with satisfaction, and slipped the plate under a magazine on the table beside her. "If you don't keep them under wraps, the nurses will think I'm sharing." She gave Tyler a wink.

His deep laughter filled the room. "You don't have to share them if you don't want to. Merry Christmas."

"Merry Christmas. Thank you, both."

Beth leaned in as they pushed the cart back toward the door and whispered, "I'm not the only one with the super power to make people smile."

"Wait a minute!" They paused, wondering if they'd forgotten something. When they looked at the woman, she pointed at the doorway above them. "Mistletoe." Her eyes glittered with amusement. "I had my grandson hang it, I have to amuse myself one way or another." She tilted her head toward them. "You're not going to disappoint an old lady during the Christmas season, are you?"

Tyler reached for Beth's hand and squeezed it gently. "We wouldn't dream of it." He turned to look at Beth and bobbed his eyebrows a couple of times.

Beth might've laughed if she weren't nervous. She'd daydreamed about their kisses many times… Warmth traveled up her body and into her face. See, this is why she wore green instead of red. There was no time to worry about how she should respond as Tyler's lips covered hers. It was a kiss that lasted maybe a moment or two too long for a simple mistletoe kiss before he stepped back again.

The older woman clapped her hands and

laughed. "Now that's the way you do it. Merry Christmas, you two."

"Merry Christmas!" They waved at her as they pushed the cart back into the hallway. Neither of them said a word until they got into the safe confines of the elevator. Beth wasn't sure whether it was a good thing or bad that they had the space to themselves. She pushed the button for the first floor and the elevator began to move.

"For the record?" Tyler's voice, slightly gruffer than usual, brought Beth's gaze to his. "I've missed that. A lot."

Oh yeah, she had, too. Beth's breath caught, her pulse thrumming in her ears. It hit her all at once. She'd fallen for Tyler. Hard. Beth shook her head and tried to pinpoint when it happened. But she couldn't, because it'd happened a little at a time. Like when he brought her lunch at work or kissed her breathless during their fishing trip. He'd even still wanted her to come celebrate Meg's birthday after Beth pushed him away. Then there were the flowers and note. Tonight, he'd taken delivering cookies to people and turned it into something she'd never forget.

It'd only been two months, but somehow, he'd managed to reach every corner of her heart.

What was it with Beth and her inability to see the big picture when it came to men? How was she supposed to protect her heart now when it already belonged to someone else?

Chapter Sixteen

Tyler waited for their cart to be loaded up with more plates of cookies. Beth was talking to someone she knew, and he couldn't take his eyes off her. From the Santa hat on her head and colorful Christmas light earrings to the green satiny dress that hugged her curves, she exuded the holiday spirit. It was no wonder she could get patients to smile and her friends to laugh.

She had a way with people.

She had a way with him.

He thought about their kiss under the mistletoe with satisfaction. It'd been a short one—way too short—but she'd leaned into him and kissed him back. There was still a lot that had to be worked out between them. Beth needed to feel comfortable enough to share the past about her ex before they could move forward.

But they were good together, of that he had no doubt.

"Okay, you guys are good to go. Here's your list for the fifth floor." One of the volunteer coordinators handed a piece of paper to Tyler. "After that, it looks like all of the plates will have been delivered. Check in when you drop off the cart to make sure."

Tyler smiled. "You've got it." He touched Beth's arm, noting the chill bumps that covered her skin. She gave the person she was speaking with a wave and turned toward him. "We've got our refill. Do you need your sweater?" He started to reach for it, but she shook her head.

"I'll be okay once we're moving again. It's chilly down here because the outside doors keep letting all the cold air in." She crossed her arms and held them close to her body.

He fought the incredible temptation to pull her into his arms and hold her until she was no longer chilled. The almost wary look on her face told him it wouldn't be a good idea. There was something about her that shifted between the last trip and this one. He couldn't quite put his finger on what it was, though. "Then let's get you moving. We're going to the fifth floor this time." He wondered what the odds were that any other patients had hung mistletoe in their doorways.

Thirty minutes later, they'd delivered all their cookies, checked in with one of the coordinators downstairs, and were heading out to the parking lot. Beth pulled her sweater closed in front to ward off the chill in the air.

"I wish we'd driven over together so I could take you home." Tyler hadn't realized he'd spoken his thoughts until the words were out. When Beth didn't reply, he started kicking himself for not having better control over his tongue. He spotted her car and walked her to it.

When they got there, Beth used her key fob to unlock it then spun on her heels to face him. "You and your family should come over for Christmas."

His eyes widened. That was about the last thing he expected. "What?"

"It's just an invitation, you can turn it down, but we're having everyone over to my parents' house for Christmas, and I thought it'd be fun if you, Meg, and your dad came, too." The whole time she spoke, she kept her gaze trained on her hands clasped in front of her.

Tyler's pulse picked up tempo. He used a finger to gently lift her chin until her eyes were on him. "I need to talk to Dad, but I'd love to spend Christmas with you, Beth." The magnetism between them was so strong, it took some serious willpower to keep from kissing her. The relief and hope in her eyes only made it harder. He ran his thumb over the soft skin of her chin before dropping his hand.

Beth drew her lower lip in between her teeth. "I'll text you with the time and all the details this week."

"Text, call, or come by the garage. Whichever is easiest for you." He wanted to ask her if he could see her between now and then, but didn't want to push his luck. "Tonight was fun, I'm glad I signed up."

"I'm glad you did too." She chuckled. "I'll warn you. You're on Lexi's list now. Expect her to ask if you want to volunteer again next year."

"If it's with you, there's a good chance I'll say yes."

It was dark outside, but the powerful lights in the parking lot lit things up well enough for Tyler to see Beth's pretty blues dilate a little. He had to get out of there before he kissed her breathless. He cupped her elbow with one hand and brushed his lips against her cheek. "Goodnight, Beth. Be safe getting home."

"I will." She ducked into her car, buckled up, and started the engine. With a final wave, he watched her car make its way through the parking lot.

Tyler exhaled slowly then grinned. Tonight had been perfect, right down to the invitation to join Beth for Christmas.

~

"Watch me, Daddy!" Meg's words filtered through the sound of the engine in the car her dad was working on.

Tyler held up one finger to get her to wait as he tried to finish what he was focused on. Several more attempts from her to get his attention passed before he looked up.

She'd balanced her large stuffed giraffe on a swiveling chair. When she saw she had his attention, she spun the chair with all her might. The animal wobbled and then launched into one of the cabinets nearby. Meg looked at him expectantly.

"Wow! Poor Mr. Speckles."

Meg giggled. "It's a ride at the fair. Do you want to see it again?"

"Sure, baby, then I've gotta get back to this."

"Okay."

Tyler watched again as the giraffe flew through the air. Poor Meg was obviously bored. It was Friday, and she had the day off from school to start the Christmas break. Tyler wished he could've had the day off to spend with her, too, but they were closing the garage for several days. Usually work slowed down quite a bit until the new year, too. Meg needed to entertain herself through today, and then he'd have a lot of time to spend with her.

Tomorrow, they'd go to the grocery store with the rest of the last-minute crowd. Tyler had a list from Dad with the ingredients they needed for the dishes they were taking for Christmas.

Merely the thought of spending that day with Beth and her family brought a smile to Tyler's face. Beth had sent the details on Monday. Since then, while he hadn't seen her, he'd spoken to her once on the phone and texted a couple of times. Their conversations had centered around Christmas and even work, but it'd been wonderful to be a part of her life again.

He glanced at Meg as she pretended to share her drink with Mr. Speckles. The conversation she had with him made him chuckle.

Dad walked up behind him. "How's it going, son?"

"It's going. I was hoping to have this done by lunch, but it'll take a while longer."

"I'm thinking burgers and fries are in order today. I'll go pick them up." He turned to Meg. "Do you want to come with me?"

Meg thought about it for a few minutes. "No, I'm going to stay with Daddy and Mr. Speckles."

"All right." Dad gave her a quick kiss. "I'll be back in a few minutes. Behave yourself." He gave her a wink and left.

Tyler made sure she was settled playing again before turning his attention to the vehicle. A few minutes later, he heard again, "Daddy! Watch this!"

"Meg, honey, I told you I need to get this

finished. Grandpa will be back with lunch soon." He kept his focus on what he was doing. Seconds later, there was a horrible screech of metal, a crash, and then the sound of his daughter screaming.

Tyler didn't think it was possible to move as fast as he did just then. He went from working under the hood to scooping his daughter up off the concrete floor. The swiveling chair was lying on its side, the water from her cup flowing everywhere, and Meg was holding her left arm to her chest. Tears streamed down her face as she cried.

"Meg, I need you to tell me what happened." She shook her head. "Baby, I can't help you if I don't know."

She took a shaky breath and tried to steady herself enough to respond. "I was standing on the chair." It was clear from the look on her face she knew she was doing something she wasn't supposed to. "I was spinning it to see what Mr. Speckles felt like."

Tyler didn't need to hear more. She'd spun it hard enough to put the chair off balance and send them both flying. She must've landed on her arm. When he tried to move it, she screamed again. He wanted to kick himself. If he'd turned around when she first tried to get his attention, he would've seen what she was doing and insisted she get down. If he hadn't been so buried in his work, this might not have happened.

Goodness knew his daughter had injured herself plenty of times in the past that required kisses and bandages, but this was different. Everything from the way she was reacting, including how she'd started to shake, to the way she held her arm, convinced him this was different. "All right, baby. I'm going to have to take you to the ER."

"I need Mr. Speckles." She hiccupped as she pointed to her giraffe.

Tyler leaned down and grabbed it, careful not to jostle her. The moment she had the animal in her arm, she buried her face in it.

He got her buckled into her booster seat. It wasn't until they were on the road to the hospital that he dialed Dad's number and told him what happened. "Yeah, we're on our way there now."

"I'll swing by the garage and make sure everything's closed up. I'll try to be at the hospital as quick as I can."

"Okay, Dad. I should've double checked all that on the way out."

"No, you're doing what you're supposed to do. I'll see you in a while."

Dad hung up then, and Tyler focused on suppressing his instinct to speed to the hospital. He glanced back at Meg. She'd stopped crying, but her face was pale. "You okay, baby?"

"It hurts."

The sound of her shaky voice, tiny within the confines of the vehicle, pierced him to the core. "I know. We're going to get your arm checked out, I promise."

He could see her nod from the rearview mirror. "I wish Grandpa and Beth were here."

"Me, too."

~

Beth checked the clock again. It was still barely after noon. The zoo was closed over the weekend for Christmas, which happened to fall on a Sunday. That meant Beth got both days off. She was more than ready for the break. If a watched pot never boiled, apparently a watched clock had the ability to freeze time. She wanted the work day to end so she could go home and bake cookies.

Monique laughed at her. "You got a hot date tonight or something?"

"No, just ready for the weekend." She normally loved Christmas and looked forward to it anyway. Throw in the fact that all her family was going to be there plus Tyler, Bill, and Meg, and it had the potential to be one of the best yet. Was it a crime to want to start the weekend off as early as possible? "You heading to Missouri tomorrow?"

"Yeah, I've got an early flight. You know you're going to miss me next week."

Monique took vacation time and would be gone the whole week after Christmas. "I'm sure I'll survive." She tossed her co-worker and friend a smile. "But yes, you're going to be missed. I hope you have a wonderful time."

"You, too. I expect you to text me and let me know how Christmas goes." Monique gave her a knowing look.

As if her phone knew they were talking about it, it chose that moment to ring. Beth saw who it was and answered. "Hey, Lexi."

"Hey, I only have a second. I'm at the hospital, and Tyler came into the ER with Meg. Said she fell and thinks she broke her arm. I figured you might want to know."

"I appreciate it, thank you."

"Yep, gotta run. See you tomorrow."

Beth frowned as she stared at the blank screen

on her phone.

"Everything okay?"

Monique's voice brought Beth's head up. "Meg fell and probably broke her arm. Tyler took her to the hospital."

"You should go."

Beth looked around the gift shop. "I can't leave you here alone."

"Are you kidding? We've had four customers all day, I think I can handle it. I'll tell the boss you had a family emergency." She winked. "Seriously, go see if there's anything you can do to help."

"Thanks, girl." Beth gave her a quick hug. "Have a safe trip and a wonderful Christmas."

"Merry Christmas to you, too!"

Beth got her stuff from the back and jogged to her car. Once she reached the hospital and entered through the emergency room's main door, she scanned the waiting room. She spotted Bill sitting in the row of chairs facing a television on the wall. Beth crossed the room and stopped in front of him.

"Hey. My sister-in-law saw Tyler and Meg come in. Any word?"

Bill ran a hand over his face. "They could tell her arm was broken and took her down to X-ray to see how bad it is."

Beth sank into the chair next to him. "Oh, no. Poor girl." She could imagine how worried Tyler had to be right now. "Do you mind if I wait with you?"

"Not at all." Bill gave her a small smile and motioned to the TV. "It looks like we have Wheel of Fortune to keep us company. You know, Tyler used to love watching this show when he was a kid."

They lapsed into comfortable silence as they

distracted themselves with the TV. Beth tried to picture a young Tyler shouting out his answers to Wheel of Fortune categories.

A half hour later, Tyler exited the double doors near the registration area, spotted them, and came their way.

Bill stood, and Beth followed suit.

"How's my granddaughter?"

"She asked for you, Dad. Said she was worried that you'd be scared out here by yourself."

Bill chuckled. "That's my Meg. What'd they say about her arm?"

"It's broken, but she doesn't need surgery. We're waiting for someone to come in and cast it."

If Beth was worried about how Tyler would feel when he saw her, she didn't have to wait any longer. He glanced at her and reached for her hand. Beth gave a gentle squeeze in return, relieved when he didn't let go.

Tyler tugged her to his side and led the way to the double doors. Beth leaned in. "Are you sure I should go back there? I don't want to overstep my bounds."

"Are you kidding?" He nodded toward the nurse who unlocked the doors for them. "On the way here, Meg said she wished Grandpa and Beth could come with her."

Beth's eyes grew moist. That Meg would ask for her when she was in pain filled Beth's heart to overflowing. What a sweet girl. Beth blinked away the tears. The last thing she wanted Meg to see was any evidence that Beth had been crying.

She didn't expect Meg to look so tiny on the hospital bed. The little girl hugged her stuffed giraffe with her right arm while her left was held against her chest with a sling. The moment she spotted them, her eyes widened and lit up.

"Grandpa! Beth! I was wishing you were here. Do you think Santa knew and sent you as an early Christmas present?"

Tyler ran a thumb over Beth's before letting go of her hand. He chuckled as he kissed his daughter on the head. "Baby, I think it was God who answered your prayers. How are you feeling?"

Meg shrugged. "I'm okay. I want to go home. We can still have Christmas with Beth, right? Please?" Hope and worry filled her eyes.

A flash of concern went across Tyler's face before it was quickly replaced with a reassuring smile. "We'll ask the doctor when he comes in, okay?"

"Okay."

The first few notes of a lullaby came over the hospital's speaker system. Meg perked up at the sound. "What does that mean?"

Beth smiled. "It means a baby was born just moments ago."

Meg's eyes widened. "They play it for every baby ever born?"

With one hand, Tyler smoothed some of her hair. "Every baby born at this hospital."

"That's neat." The little girl yawned widely and her eyes drifted shut.

It was another half hour before someone came to cast Meg's arm. Beth had no idea how long of a process it really was. A couple hours later, they were finally on their way to the parking lot. Tyler carried Meg in his strong arms, her red cast practically glowing under the sunlight. She'd said she wanted red because it would match her Christmas dress. "I'm glad I'll still be able to have Christmas with you, Beth."

"Me too, sweetie." Beth waved goodbye to Bill who got into his car and headed home. She watched as Tyler got Meg settled in his vehicle. She turned to him once he'd shut the door. "I'd love to pick up dinner and bring it by for you all. Would that be okay?"

"That would be amazing, thank you, Beth." He kissed her on the cheek and drew her against his solid chest in a warm hug. "Thanks for being here. It means a lot."

"You're welcome. I'll drop by in about an hour."

"Bring enough so you can eat with us, okay?"

She was going to ask if he was sure, but there was no doubt about that when she looked up into his eyes. "Sure."

He released her, and the cool air swooped into the space between them. She already missed the way it felt to have his arms around her.

Chapter Seventeen

Tyler didn't grasp how hungry he was until Beth walked in with pizza and breadsticks. She said she wanted to get something she knew Meg liked. He was convinced Beth was one of the kindest, most considerate people he'd ever met. That she'd get a meal and bring it by the house at nearly nine o'clock at night spoke volumes. His heart swelled with love as he watched her get a slice of sausage pizza and place it in front of Meg with a smile.

Meg didn't complain once about her arm as they all sat around the table and ate. He figured the painkillers the doctor had given her were probably helping with that. He had more acetaminophen to give her in a while, and hopefully she'd sleep comfortably tonight. In all his childhood mishaps, Tyler never had broken a bone. He imagined it would take some getting used to for Meg to sleep with the cast on her arm.

By the time they were finished eating, Meg was beginning to droop. Beth leaned over and whispered, "I brought Meg's Christmas gift with me. Is it okay if I give it to her a couple of days early?"

"Of course." He watched as she went into the living room and came back with a large gift bag. That Beth had thought to get something for Meg warmed his heart.

She handed the gift bag to Meg. "I thought you and your Mr. Speckles could use a friend."

Even though she was clearly tired, Meg's face widened in a grin. She opened the bag and pulled out a large stuffed lion. "Oh, wow! It's the lion from the zoo. Look, Grandpa. Remember when I showed this one to you?"

"I remember." Her grandfather reached out and shook the lion's hand. "Welcome to the family, Mr. Lion."

Meg hopped out of her chair and gave Beth a one-armed hug. "Thank you, I love him!" A large yawn took her breath away. "I'm going to sleep with him tonight."

"I'm glad you like him." Beth's gaze shifted to Tyler. He mouthed a "thank you." The gift was perfect.

"Speaking of bed, I think it's time you get some rest." He knew how tired she was when she didn't even complain. "Tell Beth good night." Afterward, Tyler gave her some medication, and her grandpa volunteered to help her get changed into some pajamas.

Beth stood and began consolidating the leftover pizza and breadsticks into one box. He watched her work and dreaded the idea that she was going to leave and go home soon. He took the pizza box from her, his hands covering hers. "Thanks again for bringing dinner. I'm going to get Meg to bed here in a minute. Do you have time to hang around? It shouldn't take long, she looked like she was about to fall asleep in her pizza." He needed the chance to talk to her alone. Everything with Meg today had stirred up a huge mess of emotions.

"Of course." She smiled and released the box.

He found a spot for the pizza in the fridge then went in search of his daughter. Dad had her in a nightgown that was easy to get on and off with the cast. Dad kissed her and said goodnight before leaving the room.

Tyler was right about how tired Meg was. She stayed awake long enough for him to tuck her in— along with Mr. Speckles and his new lion friend—and sing her a song. She was asleep before he left the room.

He went through the living room to gather Meg's shoes and put them by the front door. Then he followed the sound of voices to the kitchen. As he stepped through the threshold, he found Dad and Beth working on the dishes, their backs to him. He was in time to catch the end of a conversation they were having.

"You went out of your way to help tonight. Thank you for that," Dad said as he handed her a dish to dry.

"I'm glad I could do something. I hate that Meg had such a rough day." She toweled the plate dry and set it on the counter.

Dad stopped what he was doing to face her. "I'm serious. You're a keeper, Beth, and I hope my son knows that, too." He smiled and went back to the sink.

Tyler couldn't see Beth's face to gauge her reaction. On one hand, he couldn't express how much it meant for Dad to approve of Beth like that. But on the other, what if Dad's comment had hit her wrong? Was she flattered, or did the reference to a more long-term possibility in their relationship scare her?

He backed out of the doorway a few feet then went through it again, walking a little louder than normal. As he entered, they both looked over their shoulders at him. Beth's expression gave nothing away of her reaction to her conversation with Dad.

"Well, Meg's fast asleep. I'll open her door again when we go to bed so we can hear her if she has any trouble tonight."

Dad nodded. "Sounds good. I'll do the same with mine." He took the cup Beth was holding. "I'll finish this up and then go take a shower to wash off the day. Thank you again for your help." He patted her hand.

Tyler motioned for her to go ahead of him into the living room. She stood, her hands clasped behind her back, as though she wasn't sure what to do.

"Would you like to sit down for a few minutes?"

"Okay." She glanced around the living room and chose one end of the couch. She crossed one long leg over the other and leaned into the corner where the back met the arm rest. "I'm glad Meg's okay, all things considered. And if she ends up too tired or in a lot of pain, I'll completely understand if you need to stick around the house Sunday."

"Knowing my girl, she isn't going to miss Christmas at your parents' house for anything." He sat down on the couch a few feet from her. It took effort to not reach for her hand. Instead, he scratched at his beard. He'd have to make a point of trimming it before Sunday. Now that he was sitting, the weight of the day and everything that happened pressed down on his shoulders. "I can't believe all this happened. It's my fault, you know."

Beth shook her head. "Accidents happen, Tyler.

You can't blame yourself for this."

He heard her words and appreciated them, but they didn't do much to relieve the guilt. "She was bored and playing in the garage while I was working. She was spinning her toys on the chair. When she wanted me to watch her, I dismissed her because I was in the middle of something. It turns out she was standing on the chair and spinning herself around." He shuddered at the memory of turning and finding his baby lying on the concrete. "If I'd taken the time to look up when she asked me to, I would've seen what she was about to do and could've stopped her." He didn't know if he'd ever be able to get the screech of metal or the sound of her screams out of his head.

"You can't blame yourself. I'm serious, if I had a dollar for every time one of my siblings told me about a niece or nephew who got hurt while doing something they shouldn't..."

He wasn't convinced, and that must have shown on his face.

"Tyler, you can pile all the guilt on yourself you want, but it will eventually weigh you down. Trust me, I know."

When he lifted his eyes to her face, the mix of emotions he saw there made him want to take away all the worries that created them in the first place.

Beth took in a deep breath and released it again. "You make mistakes. Obviously, Meg does too. It's part of being human." She paused. "You do an amazing job with her, so give yourself a little grace. You deserve it." She grew quiet, and it was clear by the look on her face that she was thinking about something else.

He reached over and ran his hand from her

elbow to her wrist. When she turned her palm over, he took it in his. "What happened, Beth?" He rubbed his thumb lightly across hers as if the motion might coax her to share her thoughts. Tyler pushed back the disappointment and concern that flooded him when he thought she wasn't going to talk. A moment later, she took a steadying breath.

"I know what it's like to let guilt eat at you from the inside. I don't want that for you, Tyler." She briefly met his gaze before focusing on their joined hands. "I thought I knew my ex-boyfriend. I trusted him and, at one point, even wondered if he might be the one. You know?" She shook her head. "I took him home, introduced him to my family. My mom wasn't real sure about him, but everyone else thought he was great. So did I." Beth withdrew her hand and ran her fingers through her hair. "But I only knew the guy he wanted me to know. About nine months into the relationship, he started getting mean. He'd yell at me if I was late meeting him somewhere, or if I didn't return a phone call or text right away."

Tyler had a good idea where this was going. It took all his strength not to ball his hands into fists or demand to know the guy's last name and where he could find him. Instead, he remained quiet, giving Beth the time she needed.

"I always heard of women who were in abusive relationships and wondered how they could stay with the guy. I didn't get it, but I do now. Sometimes it's like a pot of cold water that warms slowly, and you don't comprehend the temperature change until it's too late." Her cheeks turned pink. "That's how it was with Carl. He was great, until he wasn't. The shift between his two personalities was subtle enough, I guess I didn't see it until it got bad."

Tyler's heart squeezed as Beth's chin dropped, but not before he spotted the tears gathering in her eyes. "What'd he do to you, Beth?"

~

A solitary tear fell, landing on one leg of Beth's blue jeans. The fabric darkened as it absorbed the liquid. Only her family knew what Carl had done. What if she told Tyler and he thought she was weak? Or worse yet, that she'd done something to make Carl treat her the way he had? A big part of her wanted to leap from the couch and run for the front door as fast as she could.

Tyler watched her, patient and understanding. He didn't push her or turn away. He was simply there, waiting, as if he'd be okay no matter what decision she made.

Suddenly, the need to tell someone—to tell him—what happened buried all her reservations. With a deep breath, she focused on the string coming from the seam of her jeans. "We were supposed to meet and go to dinner one night, but several coworkers were sick, and I didn't have a choice but to work late. I called and left a message on his phone. When I got off work, he met me in the parking lot. He yelled at me and called me horrible names like he'd been doing for a while when he got angry. Then he backhanded me."

One of her hands drifted to her right cheek. She could still feel the pain, both physical and emotional. At the time, she couldn't believe he'd actually hit her. He'd almost seemed shocked himself at the time. "He busted my lip and bruised my cheek. That's when I knew it had to end."

Beth looked at Tyler out of the corner of her eye. He clenched his jaw, a muscle in his neck bulging. What was he thinking? She wished he'd say something. Anything.

He finally released a lungful of air. "I'm sorry that happened to you. Men who think it's okay to treat a woman like that..." He took a breath. "To treat *you* like that..." He seemed at a loss for words. "Did you press charges?"

Shame, regret, and frustration all tumbled over each other and made Beth's stomach lurch. "No." She could still hear the way Carl had fallen all over himself apologizing for what happened and saying it wasn't his fault. "He said he didn't mean to, and that it would never happen again."

It was clear by the anger and sadness on Tyler's face that he knew it didn't end there. To his credit, he said nothing.

Beth appreciated the time to gather her courage to tell the rest of the story. Looking back, she couldn't believe that she'd taken Carl at his word. Whenever she thought over her decision to give him the benefit of the doubt, she wanted to travel back in time and give herself a powerful shake. "He was great for a while, and I almost forgot about what happened. Then one Friday, he came to pick me up for a date we'd set up. I quickly realized he was drunk, and he refused when I offered to drive. When I told him that I wouldn't ride with him, he became furious." He'd clenched his fists while his eyes flashed fire. "I was walking back to my house and Carl grabbed my hair—" She swallowed hard, her eyes filling with tears as the memory she tried to keep repressed pushed its way to the surface of her mind. "He threw me to the pavement, and I broke my wrist." She flexed her right hand as she remembered the pain that had radiated up her arm.

Tyler's shook his head in anger as he seemed to force himself to relax his hand so he could reach for hers. "Beth, I'm sorry."

"That's when I pressed charges." She took in a steadying breath. "He had no prior record, so he was charged with a Class A misdemeanor and fined. But Lance and Tuck—that's his best friend on the police department here—made sure Carl knew, in no uncertain terms, that he was to leave and not come back to Kitner." After swiping a finger under each of her eyes, she gave a dry chuckle. "I haven't seen him since." She'd had no doubt they'd make good on their threats if Carl came back to town, and it seemed her ex knew to take them seriously as well.

Tyler gave a decisive nod. "You were brave, Beth, to stand up to him, walk away, and file charges against him. Not everyone would be that strong." It was clear he'd meant for his words to make her feel better.

Instead, she felt numb. As though she were sinking in a pool of sticky syrup and even though someone offered her a way to climb out, she couldn't get her arms to move. How was she supposed to explain that to him? "I wasn't brave enough. It's my fault it got that far because I was stupid and give him a second chance. I knew better, but it's because I didn't have enough courage to walk away that I got hurt again." She lifted her chin and studied his face. His eyes held sadness and compassion, but there was no pity, and for that she was thankful. "Yes, he's to blame for the horrible things he said. Hurting me was completely his fault." She paused. "But I put myself in that position in the first place. I was oblivious to who he really was, and that *was* my responsibility." Surely Tyler knew she was right. Her gaze dropped to the floor.

"No." That one word was so forceful, it made Beth jump. With her attention still on the carpet, she could feel Tyler turn, put one knee up on the couch, and then take both of her hands in his. "It was not your fault. You didn't see it because you're a kind person who looks for the best in others. You didn't expect it because you treat everyone with respect and had no reason to think that wouldn't be returned." He paused. "Look at me, Beth." She sniffed and raised her head, another tear escaping and rolling down her cheek. "The fault rests solely with Carl. Don't take any of that burden on yourself because he doesn't deserve it and neither do you." One corner of his mouth lifted as he touched her cheek with his thumb, gently wiping the tear away.

The bands of dread and guilt that had been wrapped around her heart loosened a little. A sense of relief rushed in and slowly filtered through her system.

Tyler squeezed her hand. "Do you remember telling me that I should give myself some grace?"

Beth squeezed her eyes closed and nodded.

"God's got more than enough to go around. I think it's time we both followed your advice. Don't you agree?"

Give herself grace? She hadn't even thought of that. She'd been too intent on not letting her horrible experience with Carl repeat itself. She'd thought she was doing the right thing by holding on to what happened. It's what reminded her to be careful, to not let herself be duped by someone again.

Maybe Tyler was right.

She straightened her spine and squared her shoulders before opening her eyes again. "I'll try." What if she never could let go of what happened completely? The worry must have shown on her face because Tyler put his hands on her shoulders and leaned in.

"What happened to you isn't something you just get over, but I hope and pray that the effects of what he did will lessen as time goes on." He smiled, and the kindness in his eyes further eased the pain in her heart. "Every time you second-guess yourself, I'll be here to remind you how amazing you are."

His arms went around her then, and she allowed herself to sink into his chest. Into the warmth, acceptance, and comfort she found in his embrace.

Footsteps brought their attention to Bill as he entered the room. Beth let out a broken chuckle as she quickly swiped the remnants of tears from her face. She leaned away from Tyler, thankful for the darker room that was hopefully hiding her embarrassment.

To Bill's credit, he didn't even blink. "I checked on Meg again, and she's still fast asleep."

"I'm glad." Beth stood from the couch and smoothed the bottom of her shirt. "The poor thing's got to be exhausted. It's getting late, I'd better go." She looked to Tyler. "Will you please text me in the morning and let me know how she's doing?"

"Of course." He stood as well. "I'll walk you out."

Bill put a hand on Beth's shoulder. "Thanks for everything you did today, honey. We appreciate you." He gave her a kind smile. "Be careful driving home."

"I will. Thanks, Bill." She gathered her things.

Tyler escorted her through the front door to the driver's side of her car.

When they got there, he surprised Beth by pulling her into another hug. His arms wrapped around her waist, his cheek resting against hers. "It means a lot that you came by the hospital to check on Meg." He leaned his head back to see her face. "And that you told me about what happened with Carl."

The glow from the porchlight up the walkway was enough to illuminate Tyler's face. There was no missing the spark in his eyes that spoke of relief, appreciation, and something else. It bolstered her heart rate and gave her chill bumps all at the same time.

"I'm glad Meg's going to be okay." She hesitated. "Thanks for listening tonight. Outside of my family, I've never told anyone else about that."

"Then I'm honored to be that one." His breath fanned her cheek as he leaned in, his lips only an inch away from hers. "I can't wait to spend Christmas with you."

She opened her mouth to respond, and Tyler closed the gap. His lips, warm and inviting, covered hers in a kiss that sent shivers coursing down her spine and turned her legs to jelly. She hooked an arm around his neck and leaned into him to keep herself standing. Everything about the kiss—from the way his scent surrounded her to the feel of his short beard against her skin—guaranteed an extended moment she'd never forget.

When the kiss ended, Beth let her forehead rest against his shoulder. He held her close, his chin on her head. This was perfect. She wished she never had to leave the safety and comfort of his arms. *I love you, Tyler.* If she spoke the words aloud, what would he say?

Before she had a chance to convince herself either way, Tyler took a step back.

"You'd better get home and get some rest. I'll call you tomorrow." He swept some hair away from her face and tucked it behind one ear, a slow smile spreading across his face. "And I'll see you on Sunday."

Sunday. It couldn't come fast enough.

Chapter Eighteen

Tyler sprayed Meg's hair with some detangler before using the brush to work the snags out. Meg sat on the wide bathroom counter facing the mirror, a Christmas clippie in one hand and the necklace he'd given her for Christmas in the other. She'd complained little about her broken arm, except to say it was a little itchy inside. His girl was a trooper, there was no doubt about that.

"How much longer until we leave?" Meg met his eyes in the mirror, her little face full of excitement.

He glanced at his watch. "We'll carry the food out to the car in about forty minutes."

She had her legs crisscrossed in front of her, the skirt of her red Christmas dress carefully arranged over her knees, and barely sat still as he continued to brush her hair. "I can't wait. I think this is going to be the best Christmas ever."

Tyler thought so, too. "Why do you say that, baby?"

"Because we'll get to spend it with Grandpa, and

Beth, and all of her family. It's going to be so much fun. Do you think we can spend the night there?"

Tyler chuckled. "No, we're not going to spend the night." He put the brush down and held a hand out for the clippie. "Beth is pretty awesome, isn't she?" Thinking about her and that amazing kiss they shared had his heart rate soaring through the roof.

She watched him pin a little of her hair back with a clippie. "Yeah. You love her."

Tyler paused. He knew he was in love with Beth and suspected Dad knew, but he had no idea Meg had picked up on it. "Why do you say that?"

"Because I love her, too. And Grandpa says you and me are just alike." She said it so matter-of-factly that Tyler could do nothing but grin.

"Yeah, I love her. I think she's good for us, don't you?"

"Uh-huh." Meg seemed satisfied with her hair. She scrambled to get down from the cabinet. Like a little lady, she smoothed out her skirt and then handed him the necklace. "Will you put this on me, please? I can't wait to show it to everyone."

Tyler scooped her hair to the side and fastened the tiny heart necklace at the nape of her neck. Meg held it gently with two fingers and smiled at it. "I think this is my favorite present." She grinned at him.

He was glad she liked the gift. Since they'd exchanged presents that morning, Tyler had only one gift to take with him: The one he'd bought for Beth. It sat on the kitchen table, wrapped in red and gold paper, waiting for him to grab it before they left.

"I'm going to go get my shiny black shoes." She took off for her bedroom and called over her shoulder, "I'll be right back!"

It'd be difficult to keep her occupied until it was time to leave. Tyler looked at his own reflection in the mirror. He'd trimmed his beard and mustache. He ran his fingers through his hair, turned his head, and caught Meg watching him once she returned. "What do you think? Do I look nice enough for Christmas dinner?" He'd chosen a dark green sweater to wear with his black slacks. The cold temperatures and early frost guaranteed he wouldn't be too warm.

"You look handsome, Daddy." She beamed up at him then held Mr. Speckles out. "Can I take him with us? Please, please, please?"

He raised his brows. "He can come in the car, but you don't need to bring him into the house. He'll get lost and that would be a horrible way to end Christmas. Don't you think?"

Meg stuck her lower lip out for a second or two before nodding thoughtfully. "Yeah, he might get sad." She turned the giraffe to look at her. "You'll have to wait for me in the car. I'll save a cookie for you." She smiled at Tyler before running off again.

"Whoa, little lady. Watch where you're going."

"Sorry, Grandpa!"

Dad appeared in the doorway. "To be a kid again on Christmas." He chuckled. "You clean up good, son."

"Thanks. You do too." Tyler nodded his approval at Dad's choice of button-up red shirt. As he observed their reflections in the mirror, he was reminded how much they favored each other.

Meg's voice filtered in from the living room. "Daddy? Is it time to go yet?"

Tyler laughed. "I'm not sure she's going to survive waiting much longer."

"Then we'll load up the car and drive down some streets to look at Christmas lights on our way there."

Now that was a great idea. By the time they had everything in the 4Runner, they didn't have a whole lot of time to kill anyway. Dad drove, and Tyler was content to sit in the passenger seat and admire the Christmas lights with his family.

His thoughts drifted to Beth. He was starting to automatically include her in with his family now, and nothing had ever felt more right.

~

To say Beth's parents' house was full to the brim was a huge understatement. The house was already crowded, and they were still missing Lance and Lexi as well as Tyler and his family. Mom joked about how they might have to rent a recreation center or something next year, but the contented look on her face said it all: She was loving every minute of it.

Beth passed the front window for the third or fourth time and looked through the glass. This time, she saw Tyler's 4Runner park along the curb. She ping-ponged between feeling giddy and nervous. Giddy because she couldn't wait to see him and spend the holiday with him. Nervous because she didn't know what to expect after the other night. She didn't have to wonder long, though. Bill gave her a hug, and Meg twirled in her pretty dress before launching herself into Beth's arms. When Meg skipped off to play with the many other children in the house, Beth turned to find Tyler watching her, approval written all over his face. Dressed in slacks and a nice sweater, he looked like he'd stepped right out of a magazine.

He took her hand and kissed her on the corner of her mouth. "You look gorgeous. Merry Christmas, sweetheart."

The term of endearment made her heart skip a beat and brought a smile to her face. "Merry Christmas."

Introductions started then, and there were a lot of them. Beth doubted poor Tyler and his family would remember half of the people they met. She was happy to see that Meg seemed to fit right in with the other children.

Tyler pointed to the group of kids who were sitting on the floor admiring trading card collections and other toys. "This is good for her. There's nothing wrong with being an only child, but I sometimes feel bad that she doesn't even have cousins to play with." His eyes flitted to one of the boys who was sitting a little apart from the others. "Now, whose son is that?"

Beth smiled. "That's Gideon. Serenity is Lexi's younger sister and that's her boy. Serenity and Aaron got married earlier this year, and Aaron adopted him." Gideon looked up when someone said his name and smiled. "He has autism, and he's done well over the last couple of years. That he's over there by the other kids is huge."

Someone tapped on her shoulder. Beth stood and turned to find Lexi's grandmother standing behind her. "Merry Christmas, Grams! It's been a while since I've seen you." She gave the older woman a hug.

"It sure has. Have you met my new husband?" Grams hooked an arm through the gentleman's elbow at her side. "This is Peter Quintin."

"Of course! I heard about your wedding, congratulations to the both of you." She introduced them to Tyler and the men shook hands. "I need to ask Lexi to text me some of your wedding photos."

Peter leaned in and gave Grams a squeeze. "She was the most beautiful bride."

The look Grams gave him spoke of a woman madly in love. "Don't you two forget to grab a glass of eggnog. I made it myself." She winked, and they moved toward the kitchen.

"They seem really nice," Tyler said, smiling after them. "She's your grandmother?"

"No, she's Lexi's grandmother, but everyone calls her Grams."

"You'll have to tell me the story behind how she and Peter met." He nodded toward one corner of the living room. "And who is that Dad's talking to?"

It took Beth a moment to visually sift through all the people. "Oh! That's Lexi's mom, Patty." She watched as Patty and Bill talked for a bit and laughed several times. "They seem to be getting along exceptionally well. Patty's a widow, you know." She gave Tyler a knowing look.

He watched them, a look of amusement and surprise on his face. "Yeah, I'm going to have to tease Dad about this one."

Beth looked at her watch. Everyone had been at the house mingling and visiting for at least a half hour. "I wonder where Lance and Lexi are? They're usually one of the first people to arrive to anything."

"I was wondering the same thing myself." Avalon stopped nearby. "Did I tell you Lorelei hasn't put your book down since you gave it to her? You've got yourself a fan. I hope you're writing another one soon."

"I've got some more in the works." Beth had

given copies of *Zoe the Zebra to the Rescue* to all her younger nieces and nephews. These glowing reports had Beth excited to publish the next book sometime after the new year.

Avalon took her phone out of her pocket. "Seriously, though, do you think I should call Lance and make sure they're okay?"

The doorbell rang, barely audible over all the conversations. Avalon pointed to the door. "I'll get it." She mimicked swimming motions as she made her way through the crowd, drawing chuckles from those around her.

She opened the door to reveal Lance on the other side. He wore a sheepish expression on his face as he stepped just inside the door. "Sorry we're late everyone."

"You're lucky I didn't eat all the cookies!" Tuck hollered from the middle of the room. Everyone laughed.

"I promise we have a good reason." Lance's face transformed into a brilliant grin tinged with pride. He turned sideways to clear the doorway. Lexi stepped forward, a tiny bundle in her arms. She pushed a corner of the blue blanket back to reveal a baby's sleeping face. "Lexi and I would like to introduce you to our son, Jacob Robert." He put a hand on the tiny head covered with black hair. "Jacob, this huge mess of people is your family."

Beth's hand flew to her mouth, her eyes instantly flooded with tears. Tyler stood with her and leaned in close. "I'm missing something."

She filled him in as quickly as she could, brushing at her tears as she told him how badly her brother and sister-in-law wanted children. "This is a Christmas miracle."

After waiting for what felt like forever, it was finally her turn to see the new baby. How the little guy still slept through everything was beyond Beth. Then again, he'd remained cradled in his mommy's arms. It didn't look like Lexi had any desire to relinquish her new baby boy anytime soon.

"He's beautiful. Absolutely beautiful. I'm unbelievably happy for you two." Beth hugged Lance tight before giving Lexi a more careful hug. Her eyes widened with realization. "Was this why you were at the hospital on Friday?"

Lexi nodded and laughed through her tears. "Yes, he was born probably an hour after I called you. It was hard not to tell everyone, but we wanted to wait until we were all together today."

Beth reached out and touched the baby's hand with a finger. "You have no idea how long your mommy and daddy have prayed to meet you, Jacob. Never doubt how loved you are." Another tear rolled down her cheek, but Beth didn't care. The baby scrunched his face a little and whimpered before settling back into a peaceful sleep.

As much as Beth wanted to stand there and stare at her new nephew, there were other family members who couldn't wait for their chance to see him. Beth stepped away, swiping at her tears. She glanced at Tyler and laughed. "Now you know my secret: I can be a little sentimental."

"Come here." Tyler pulled her into a tight hug. "In case you ever wondered, you look beautiful even when you're crying."

Beth giggled into his shirt and relished the feel of his arms around her. Best. Christmas. Ever.

~

After four hours of Christmas festivities at the Davenport home, everyone was starting to slow down a little. Tyler didn't think he could eat another bite until Beth walked up with a plate in his hand. "Fudge?"

Who turns down a piece of fudge? Yeah, no sane person. "Thanks." He polished it off in two bites. "I may not eat for a week after this."

"Me, either." Beth raised an eyebrow and took a bite. "Marian makes the best fudge. She mailed me some for my birthday once, and I kept it in the fridge and managed to make it last almost three months."

She wasn't kidding about the fudge. "I'm impressed. It wouldn't last that long at my house." He took her free hand and placed a kiss to her knuckles. "Wait here a minute." He retrieved his gift for her that he'd stashed with their coats.

Beth put the plate down, surprise on her face. "What's this?"

"It's your Christmas present." He handed it to her. "Open it."

She smiled and carefully pulled the paper away. When the leather journal was exposed, she ran a finger over the engraved butterfly on the cover. "It's beautiful, Tyler."

He'd thought of Beth the moment he'd seen the journal last week. "I figured you could use it to jot down book ideas and things like that when you didn't have your computer available. Or you could use it to confess your deepest secrets." He tossed her a grin. "Whichever you'd prefer."

Beth stood on tip toe and kissed him briefly.

"Thank you, it's perfect."

Tyler slipped his arms around her waist and held her close. "You're welcome."

She pulled away and smiled. "I brought something for you, too."

Now that he hadn't expected. He watched as she disappeared from the room only to return a minute later. She held a small, wrapped box in her hands and handed it to him. "It's a little different, but I thought it was fitting." With the journal held against her chest, she motioned for him to open it.

Tyler unwrapped the box and lifted the top. Inside was a watch with a silver band and a jaguar etched into the face. It wasn't what he expected, but she was right, it was fitting. "This is amazing, Beth. You spent way too much on this."

Beth shook her head. "I get a good discount at the gift shop." She gave him a wink and then laughed. "I thought that, since we first met at the zoo and had our first official date near the jaguars, it would be a fun gift. You don't have to wear it, though, if it's not your style."

"Are you kidding?" He slipped his old watch off and put it in his pocket before putting the new one on. "It's great."

A round of laughter exploded from the living room. Tyler glanced toward them and chuckled. "Your family is amazing. It's been fun getting to see what a big Christmas gathering is like."

Beth looked over her shoulder and smiled fondly. "Yeah, they're alright most of the time."

Tyler glanced above them and grinned. "Hey, did you see where we're standing?"

She looked confused until she raised her chin and

spotted the mistletoe hanging from the ceiling. "How did I not see that before? I swear, you just put it there, didn't you?"

He held up both hands. "I promise, I didn't."

She raised one eyebrow in a way that made her look absolutely adorable. He took one large step forward and looked down into her face. "I, for one, have no intention of letting some good mistletoe go to waste."

Beth giggled as his lips covered hers in the kind of kiss he'd been waiting all evening for. Everything around them faded away and there was nothing except for the feel of Beth in his arms and the way their hearts seemed to beat as one.

And then there were the whistles and catcalls.

Tyler broke their kiss to find Beth's face turning pink before she hid it against the front of his shirt. She lifted her head again and gave a little wave to their audience, starting up another round of laughter.

"Well, you wanted to see what life was like with a big extended family." She motioned toward the living room. "There you have it, in a nutshell. Have they scared you away yet?"

"Not even close." He caressed the soft skin along her jaw. "I love everything about you, Beth."

She wrinkled her nose a little, her eyes twinkling. "Yeah?"

"Mmmmhmmmm." He placed a light kiss to the tip of her nose.

"I'm head over heels in love with you, too."

Tyler smiled with a groan. "You have no idea how badly I want to kiss you again. If only we didn't have an audience."

"You kidding? I say we give them something to

whistle about." She flashed him a mischievous grin.

That was all Tyler needed. His lips found hers in a heartbeat as he gathered Beth in his arms and kissed her with all the love he had to offer.

Epilogue

heck this out, Mama!" Meg's voice called out from the living room.

Beth still loved it every time Meg called her that. She remembered with clarity the first night she tucked Meg in after she and Tyler got married. Meg had said she'd always wanted a mommy and that God had finally answered her prayers. Even thinking about it now brought tears to Beth's eyes.

She slid the pan of muffins into the oven, set the timer, and followed the sound of her girls laughing.

When Beth entered the room, Meg was crawling around on all fours. Meanwhile, two-year-old Molly squealed with delight as she sat on her sister's back and held onto her shirt. "Go, horsie, go!"

Beth laughed. "Don't let go, Molly."

"Oh, she's holding on tight." Meg turned her head slightly to look at Beth. She made an exaggerated grab at her neck where her shirt was being pulled against it. "Almost too tight." At nearly ten-years-old, Meg had no problem supporting her little sister's weight. She pretended to whinny and took off at an even faster speed, resulting in a round of giggles from her little passenger.

Beth was smiling at the antics of her two beautiful daughters when Tyler came up behind her and slipped his arms around her waist. She loved it when he held her like this. Beth leaned into his solid chest. "When did they get so big? Look at them! Molly's not a baby anymore."

"I don't know. I wish they wouldn't grow up this fast, though." He chuckled. "You know, if you're missing the baby stage..." He nuzzled her neck, making Beth squirm.

She turned in his arms to face him. "Are you serious?" They'd talked about having several kids before Molly was born, but the subject hadn't come up in a while.

"Why not? Molly's almost potty trained." He smiled as he tucked some hair behind her ear. "Besides, it'll be fun." He waggled his eyebrows at her.

Beth smacked him on the arm. "Tyler!"

"Watching three kids playing in the living room would be fun. What did you think I meant?" The mischievous glint in his eye told her he knew exactly what he'd said.

She shook her head at him. "You're something else, you know that?" She paused. "Maybe the next one will be a boy."

Tyler pulled her close. "Maybe so." He smiled. "If not, we can try again." He kissed her. "And again." Another kiss had Beth chuckling against his lips.

Molly slipped off Meg's back and both girls collapsed on the floor in giggles.

"Seriously, though." Tyler nodded toward their

daughters. "I like having a houseful of girls. Especially when they're as sweet and pretty as their mom."

The timer rang in the kitchen as he gave her a brief, but thorough, kiss. "I love you."

"I love you, too." Beth smiled into his dark eyes.

"Mama, the timer went off. Does that mean the muffins are ready?"

Beth looked down into the hopeful faces of her daughters. "You bet they are. Who's up for a snack?"

"Me!"

"I am!"

Tyler took Beth's hand as they followed the girls into the kitchen. "You know what?"

"What's that?" She looked over at him.

"I like us," he said with that sweet smile that always made her heart melt.

"I like us, too."

Thank you!

I appreciate you for taking the time to read **Finding Grace**. I hope you enjoyed it and that you'll consider leaving a review on Amazon and/or Goodreads. I like hearing what you think about it and it'll help other readers discover new books as well.

Acknowledgments

Doug, Xander, and Sydney, I couldn't have written this series without you all. You've been my inspiration, my support, and you've kept me grounded. Seriously, thank you for the joy you all bring into my life each day. I love you!

Crystal, it's weird to think that you and I weren't yet critique partners when I started this series. A lot has changed in three years, and I'm so thankful that we met! As always, your advice has been invaluable. Here's to walking through this journey together, my friend.

You did it again, Vicki. I couldn't love this book cover more. Thank you for always creating beautiful covers that I look forward to sharing with my readers.

Krista, thank you for not only editing my baby here, but giving me some advice on ways to make her even better.

Many thanks to my supportive critique group: Vicki, Kris, Rachel, Franky, and Amy. From your great suggestions to helping me get the wording on the blurb just right, your opinions are always valuable.

My beta readers are awesome. Sending out a big thank you to Steph, Mom (Suzanne), Denny, and Sandy. You ladies have eagle eyes, and I appreciate you!

This series wouldn't be what it is without all of you wonderful readers. Thank you for sticking with me as we got to know the Chandler and Davenport families.

It's been an amazing ride!

Most of all, I want to thank my heavenly Father. When I first wrote *Finding Peace*, I had no idea what the future had in store for me. He's led me on an adventure that surpassed everything I could've hoped for. To Him be the glory!

About the Author

Melanie D. Snitker has enjoyed writing fiction for as long as she can remember. She started out creating episodes of cartoon shows she wanted to see as a child, and her love of writing grew from there. She and her husband live in Texas with their two children, who keep their lives full of adventure, and two dogs, who add a dash of mischief to the family dynamics. In her spare time, Melanie enjoys photography, reading, crocheting, baking, and hanging out with family and friends.

www.melaniedsnitker.com
https://twitter.com/MelanieDSnitker
www.facebook.com/melaniedsnitker

Subscribe to Melanie's newsletter and receive a monthly e-mail containing recipes, information about new releases, giveaways, and more! You can find a link to sign up on her website.

Books by Melanie D. Snitker

Calming the Storm
(A Marriage of Convenience)

Love's Compass Series:
Finding Peace (Book 1)
Finding Hope (Book 2)
Finding Courage (Book 3)
Finding Faith (Book 4)
Finding Joy (Book 5)
Finding Grace (Book 6)

Life Unexpected Series:
Safe In His Arms (Book 1)
Someone to Trust (Book 2)

Brides of Clearwater Series:
Marrying Mandy (Book 1)

Welcome to Romance:
Finding Forever in Romance

Made in the USA
Columbia, SC
16 January 2018